HER RIVAL'S TOUCH

AN ISLAND OF YS NOVEL

KATEE ROBERT

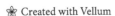 Created with Vellum

To all the Liam fans out there.
This one is for you.

ALSO BY KATEE ROBERT

The Island of Ys
Book 1: His Forbidden Desire
Book 2: Her Rival's Touch

The Thalanian Dynasty Series (MMF)
Book 1: Theirs for the Night
Book 2: Forever Theirs
Book 3: Theirs Ever After
Book 4: Their Second Chance

The Kings Series
Book 1: The Last King
Book 2: The Fearless King

The Hidden Sins Series
Book 1: The Devil's Daughter
Book 2: The Hunting Grounds
Book 3: The Surviving Girls

The Make Me Series
Book 1: Make Me Want
Book 2: Make Me Crave
Book 3: Make Me Yours
Book 4: Make Me Need

The O'Malley Series
Book 1: The Marriage Contract

Book 2: The Wedding Pact

Book 3: An Indecent Proposal

Book 4: Forbidden Promises

Book 5: Undercover Attraction

Book 6: The Bastard's Bargain

The Hot in Hollywood Series

Book 1: Ties that Bind

Book 2: Animal Attraction

The Foolproof Love Series

Book 1: A Foolproof Love

Book 2: Fool Me Once

Book 3: A Fool for You

Out of Uniform Series

Book 1: In Bed with Mr. Wrong

Book 1.5: His to Keep

Book 2: Falling for His Best Friend

Book 3: His Lover to Protect

Book 3.5: His to Take

Serve Series

Book 1: Mistaken by Fate

Book 2: Betting on Fate

Book 3: Protecting Fate

Come Undone Series

Book 1: Wrong Bed, Right Guy

Book 2: Chasing Mrs. Right

Book 3: Two Wrongs, One Right

Book 3.5: Seducing Mr. Right

Other Books
Seducing the Bridesmaid
Meeting His Match
Prom Queen
The Siren's Curse

CONTENT WARNING

This book contains characters with a history of childhood abuse (that is *not* described in graphic detail in the story), violence, and the threat of sexual assault.

It also contains light BDSM, a dirty talking hero, and a whole lot of sexy betting.

CHAPTER 1

*W*hen the Island of Ys was created and the Horsemen chose their monikers, there was no doubt in anyone's mind that Kenzie should be War. Hers, least of all. She was the fighter, the one who went balls to the wall in any confrontation—and usually came out on top.

She was also the one currently hiding in the staff kitchen of their casino, Pleasure.

The various cooks and servers cast her curious looks, but they knew better than to ask actual questions about why she was lurking *there* instead of literally anywhere else in Pleasure. The casino had passageways built in a warren through it so the Horsemen could move about as they pleased, and if she wanted to avoid a certain person, those passageways would be a better option.

Or they would be if they didn't house her siblings.

Kenzie sighed and poked at the plate the head chef had slammed in front of her a few minutes ago. She couldn't keep going on like this. There were things in motion that required her presence, things she should be *happy* to finally put to bed. Vengeance. Justice. The term didn't matter. What *did* matter

1

was punishing the people responsible for hurting her, her siblings, and hundreds of other innocent children.

That's what she should be focused on.

Not the man currently stalking her through Pleasure's floors.

She sighed again and bumped her head against the wall. She should just talk to him. It would dispel any notions he had about her. Liam Neale might have come to this island to... Well, she still wasn't quite sure *why* he'd come to compete in the Wild Hunt, but it didn't matter. He lost. End of story.

Or at least it should have been.

The phone on the wall next to her head rang and she cursed. No point in ignoring it. He'd just keep calling. With a third, much more dramatic sigh, she yanked the receiver down. "What?"

"Come back to the hub. You're making the kitchen staff nervous by lurking down there." Ryu. Her brother in everything but blood.

"I tried that. Amarante told me to stop hiding and deal with Liam."

Ryu paused, probably to let her think about the stupidity of the situation she now found herself in. "And yet you're still hiding, and Liam still hasn't been dealt with."

"Mmmhmm."

"Kenzie, since when do you avoid a confrontation?"

That was the question, wasn't it? If Liam was any other person, he'd have long since been hog-tied and put on a boat or helicopter off the island. But in the single conversation they'd had, she hadn't come out on top. In fact, she hadn't even been sure which way was up when she walked away from it. "Something's off about him."

"About *him*?"

"Shut it, Ryu."

He made a sound that might have been a muffled laugh. "If you don't handle him, Amarante will."

Their sister wouldn't be gentle. Not when the thing they'd worked fifteen long years to accomplish was finally in motion. The initial stage of their plan worked. They'd acquired the Bookkeeper who ran the money funneled into that hellhole of a camp back in the day. The woman had given them three names. Not the top of the power structure —no one seemed to know who *that* was—but three people who had actually run the day to day tortures. One of them would know the party ultimately responsible. One of them had to.

In the meantime, they would remove those three blights from the world.

As soon as they tracked them down.

They couldn't do that with Liam hanging around, sticking his nose where it didn't belong. He wasn't like the other patrons. He wasn't here to gamble or relax or indulge in the best fantasies money could buy. He stalked around like a beast in a cage, and it didn't seem to matter to him that he'd *chosen* to be there.

Ryu apparently got tired of her waffling and said, "He's making the other guests nervous, and that's bad for business. You have to get rid of him. Today."

Or Amarante would do it herself. If Liam decided to be difficult in the process, she might even do it in a more permanent way. Given the man's short track record on the island, *difficult* was his middle name.

Amarante hadn't chosen Death's role without good reason.

"Fine. I'll take care of it." She hung up and stood. Kenzie never held off once she'd decided on a course, and now was no exception. No matter how nervous he made her for reasons she refused to acknowledge, at the end of the day,

Liam was just a man, and Kenzie had dealt with men before.

She adjusted her dress—red and hugging her body in a way that made her feel ten feet tall and invincible. She paused to thank the head chef for the meal and then strode out of the kitchen and down the hall to the main casino floor. Unlike their second casino on the south half of the island, Pain, this one was set up the same way casinos were around the world. Slots lined the walls and created walkways through the floor, broken up only by various other games—roulette and blackjack and craps. Several bars ensured alcohol was never too far away.

It was only window dressing, of course. People didn't travel all the way to the Island of Ys to gamble. They could do that in any other casino on the planet.

No, they came there to have their every fantasy played out.

Kenzie stopped in the middle of the floor and turned a slow circle. He was here somewhere. He was *always* here. Her skin prickled with awareness at the same moment her attention snagged on the single pool of stillness in the middle of the frenzy.

Lord, but he was something else. She could admit that to herself, if she could admit it to no one else. Liam Neale might have actually won the Wild Hunt if they hadn't hedged their bets and cheated the tiniest bit to ensure he didn't. Or, rather, to ensure the right person *did*.

He was watching her. He always seemed to be watching her, those dark eyes holding mysteries she told herself she had no interest in discovering. Dark eyes and dark hair, with skin that was more tan than when he'd arrived on the island. When he stood and started for her, he moved with a lethal kind of grace that her body responded to even as her mind called her seven different kinds of an idiot. No matter how

4

attractive the flame, dangerous men had a habit of burning those around them.

She knew that, being a dangerous woman.

The only people she'd managed to retain were her siblings, and their relationship was forged by trauma stronger than any inferno. There was nothing she could do that would make them turn their backs on her, and that knowledge kept her warm most nights. *That* was love.

Fucking, no matter how good, couldn't compare.

Not that she was thinking about fucking Liam. She certainly wasn't. Especially with him currently bearing down on her like a predator scenting blood in the water. *Damn it, Kenzie.*

She barely waited for him to get close enough to hear her over the jaunty music of the machines around them. "You have to leave."

"I haven't got what I came for yet." Even his voice was sinful, low, and rough.

"That's a shame, because you aren't going to get whatever you came for. You're leaving. Today. Now."

"No." Just that. As if he really had a say.

Kenzie propped a hand on her hip, not bothering to strive for patience. She had none. "You either do this the easy way or the hard way, but you're leaving the island."

He leaned down, just a little. Not enough to really get in her space, but enough to let her know he most definitely could if he was so inclined. "No."

"For fuck's sake, what do you *want?* It's not to gamble and it's not to fuck or any of the other things we offer here. If you're still licking your wounds over losing the Wild Hunt, sorry, not sorry, I don't care about your manly pride. I care about my bottom line, and you're affecting it. Move or I will move you."

Liam shrugged, letting that threat roll right off his broad shoulders. "You can try."

That was it. He was going to drive her to break her own rules and just flat out murder him. "What. Do. You. Want?"

For the first time since he'd arrived on the island, he actually looked less than fully in control. Surprise flickered over his expression. "You really don't remember me, do you?"

*   *   *

LIAM HAD KNOWN the truth even before he saw it reflected in Kenzie's hazel eyes. She had no memory of him. None. The night eight years ago might have been imprinted beneath his skin, but she'd walked and never spared him a second thought. Fuck, he was an idiot.

It didn't change his reason for being here.

He might have entered the Wild Hunt with the intention of securing Death's favor to find the woman who haunted his dreams all these years, but he honestly hadn't expected to arrive on the island and see *her*. What were the odds? Too impossible to put a number to.

And yet here she was.

She flipped her blond hair off her shoulder and glared up at him. "What are you on about?"

"Boston. Eight years ago. We shared a bottle of top shelf whiskey in a little hole in the wall bar and then fucked on every surface of your hotel room. And then you robbed me."

She looked at him as if seeing him for the first time, and he found himself holding his breath while he waited. That flicker of recognition in her hazel eyes died. "Sorry, you've got the wrong girl."

She does *remember me.*

I fucking knew it.

"No, I don't." He leaned forward. He couldn't help

6

himself. The siren call of her was too strong to deny. Liam lowered his voice and delivered his knockout punch. "Kenzie."

She jerked as if he'd hooked her up to a live wire. "What did you just call me?"

It proved his theory that she didn't just randomly give out her name to people—publicly she was known as War and only that—which, in turn, supported the fact that that night had meant as much to her as it had to him. "You're name. The one you told me." He should have left it there, but frustration boiled beneath his skin, a product of too many days spent inactive, within touching distance of his goal but unable to close the space between them. "While you were riding my cock for the third time."

She paled, but recovered almost instantly and cast a look at the front of his slacks. "Maybe if I saw your cock, I'd actually remember you."

Stupid to let the cut land. He'd known that it wouldn't be easy to find the mystery woman, let alone to convince her to give him a shot. She had all the information she needed in the wallet she'd stolen from him. If she wanted to find him after that, she could have.

"A conversation, Kenzie."

"Stop saying that name," she hissed.

"A conversation," he repeated. "Surely that's not too much to ask."

She frowned. "A conversation and then you leave."

"Sure," he lied easily. Now that he'd found her, he wasn't leaving until he saw this through one way or another. His best friend, Aiden, had called him an idiot for hunting the idea of a woman he'd met once, but that night was a fever in his blood that he couldn't ease. He needed to know if there was something there, or at least get some fucking closure so he could move on with his life. There had never been time for selfish pursuits, not when the O'Malley family teetered on the verge of war and needed every soldier on alert. Now they were finally at peace, which meant now he was free to pursue his dream.

To pursue Kenzie.

She finally shrugged. "Fine. I can spare five minutes."

Fuck, but this woman was harder to pin down than smoke. Even when he'd failed to win the Wild Hunt, he hadn't lost hope because now he knew where she was. Except he couldn't get to her. Every time he caught sight of her blond wave of hair, or the red she seemed to wear like a banner of war, she'd disappear before he could reach her. Like some kind of living nightmare where Liam was always a step behind and too slow to do anything about it.

This place had to be riddled with back doors and hallways the public didn't know about, because he'd never had someone slip his grasp so many times. The frustration had him going out of his skin.

He followed her through the cascade of sound the slot machines emitted. It was wasn't smoky in here like in some casinos, and the air had the faintest tinge of salt as a reminder that they weren't far from the water. A temptation to leave the four walls of this place and walk outside. Liam shook it off. He wasn't there for the same reason the other patrons were.

He was there for Kenzie.

She finally pulled open an unassuming-looking door that led into an honest to god boardroom. Liam pulled up short. "Ah."

"Not everyone comes here to play," she said. She dropped into one of the plush chairs and steepled her fingers in front of her red lips as if she was an old school mob boss about to hear a business proposal.

The irony was not lost on Liam.

He weighed his choices and finally took the chair across the table from her. From what he'd seen of Kenzie, crowding her was a good way to end up laid out. She struck out in violence as easily as she laughed, her threats interchangeable with her jokes. If he was back home in Boston, he never would have let her anywhere near the family he worked as protection for. She was too much of a threat.

"Tick tock." She looked at her empty wrist, at her nonexistent watch.

A thousand times he'd walked through what he'd say to this woman if he ever laid eyes on her again, but in the end it all boiled down to one question. "Why?"

"You'll have to be more specific."

"Why did you leave like that?"

She looked at him like he was a new kind of species she'd never seen before. "Did you really go through all this trouble to track down a woman who robbed you? How much was taken? I'll write you a check." She smirked. "Actually, since my moral character is in question, I'll just give you cash. That should clear this whole thing right up."

"Kenzie."

She slammed her hands onto the table. "For the last fucking time, do *not* call me that. My name is War, and you'll do well to remember that." She narrowed her eyes. "I don't care that you have connections to both the Irish and the Russian mob. I really don't. You're not in Boston and you're not in New York, Liam. You're on the Island of Ys, and here *we* reign supreme. If you cross me, I will bury you."

If using her name meant so much, then her giving it to him in the first place only confirmed that he was right to track her down. "It's not about the robbery and you damn well know it."

"I don't know anything of the sort." Like a flip was switched, she relaxed and leaned back in her chair, all mocking smiles and angelic features. "Let's pretend for a second that what you claim happened really *did* happen."

"It did."

She ignored him. "You can't honestly expect me to be able to recall everyone I've robbed over the years. There were..." A cloud passed over her features, some remembered darkness, but she brushed it off between one blink and the next. "My sweet, sweet boy, there were thousands."

"Did you sleep with all your marks?"

She arched her brows. "If I did, it wouldn't be any of your business. For the last time, Liam, *why are you here?*"

"I'm here for you," the words felt pulled from his chest. "I'm here for you, Kenzie."

Kenzie pushed slowly to her feet. She wore a red dress that spilled like blood down her breasts and stomach and hips, and he wasn't stupid enough to miss the warning there. He simply didn't give a fuck. The risk was worth the potential reward.

She took a step back and seemed to steel herself. "It was one night of sex. Men do not chase women across most of a decade and half the world because of a single night of sex."

I knew you remembered.

He didn't move. Didn't do anything that would spook her more than he already had. "It was more than sex."

"Don't make me laugh. I expect that kind of sentimental bullshit from some people. You should know better." She gave him an appraising look. "How many people have you killed, Liam? Lives snuffed out to secure the O'Malley power base. Men like you see the world in cold hard facts—black and white. They don't do...this." She waved a hand at the room. "For the third and final time—why are you here?"

"Why is it so hard for you to believe that I'm here for you?"

CHAPTER 2

*K*enzie clenched her fists and fought for control. Every word out of Liam's mouth battered against her defenses, dragging that long forgotten memory from the box she'd locked it away in and out into the light. A night with expensive whiskey on her lips, that taste nothing compared to the man before her. Of his rough hands on her body, his voice saying things she both loved and hated because they could have no promises between them, no matter what he seemed to want.

Of waking up the next morning and being struck by the desire to linger.

That, more than anything, had driven her from that hotel room. Taking his wallet was an impulse, spending his money evidence to prove to herself that she really hadn't been affected.

None of that mattered now.

It couldn't.

Not when they were so close to seeing their vengeance done.

Even if they *weren't*, one night of sex couldn't mean anything. Anyone could fake anything for twelve hours, the simplest of deceptions. She'd spent fifteen years pretending to be carefree, until the mask had sealed itself to her and some days she didn't know where it ended and the true Kenzie began.

She finally dragged her gaze away from him. "I don't know how this played out in your head, but even if I was willing—and I'm not—it won't be like you've apparently spent eight years imagining. You have one night built up into something that it's not. It was sex, Liam. Just outstanding sex with a side of highway robbery."

"Relationships have been started on less." The words came from closer than she expected.

She jerked back to find him on his feet. Damn it, she was better than this. She couldn't afford to be distracted with an enemy in the room—even if that enemy didn't seem to mean her harm. Kenzie knew better than to bank on that truth. Even when people didn't mean harm, their selfish tendencies still caused it to ripple from them in waves. Liam was no different.

"Relationships." She laughed. She couldn't help it. "Be honest with yourself if you can't be honest with me. You didn't chase down some woman you fucked because you're looking for a relationship."

"What will it take for you to believe me?"

"Nothing you have. Nothing you can spare." If things were different... She shut that thought down before it could take hold. Things *weren't* different, and wishing for another world was a good way to get herself and the people she cared about killed. Liam was a distraction, and Kenzie annihilated distractions as a matter of course. "Leave. If you don't, my sister will ensure that you do, and she won't be picky about whether you're walking out on your own two feet or in a body bag."

"I'm not afraid of Death."

"You should be." Amarante wouldn't waffle the way Kenzie was now. She never wavered when it came to their end goal, and that determination had kept all four of them alive in a time and place when it shouldn't have been possible. If it meant she didn't know how to bend... Well, it was a small price to pay.

Liam looked at her with those dark eyes that seemed to see too much. "What are you so afraid of?"

"I'm not afraid." The protest burst out of her lips on reflex and she cursed herself for letting even that much control slip. Kenzie and control weren't often on speaking terms, but she needed to get that impulsive part of her locked down right now.

His lips twitched. Not quite a smile. No, it was a challenge. "Prove it."

"You really think that childish taunt is going to work on me? We're not on the playground." She found herself leaning toward him, a planet to the gravity of his sun, and forced her feet flat and her back straight. What was *wrong* with her?

"Kenzie." He said her name so softly, like a caress of a single finger against her skin. "Tell me you don't remember it. Tell me that it's not *worth* remembering."

She opened her mouth to do exactly that, but the words wouldn't come. Had she forced herself to forget? Yes, of course. Over the years, Kenzie had gotten really good at packaging away things she couldn't handle thinking about. Sometimes in the darkest part of the night, they escaped and knocked her flat on her ass, but invariably the sun always rose, and relief came with the morning.

Liam wasn't one of the nightmares. It would be easier to deal with him if he was.

13

If she didn't do something, and do it fast, she would touch him. The ultimate betrayal, because Kenzie couldn't guarantee her control if she got her hands on this man. If *he* got his hands on *her*. "How about a bet?"

He frowned. "A…bet."

"Sure." She should just kick him out. Call security if she was so concerned she couldn't handle it herself… Except Kenzie couldn't do that. The Horsemen had a reputation to uphold, after all. That meant certain protocols were in place. For anyone truly dangerous, they took care of it themselves.

Liam was nothing if not dangerous.

He finally straightened and crossed his arms over his chest. "You want to bet me… What, exactly?"

"Blackjack. I win, you leave immediately."

His dark eyes flared in interest. "And if I win?"

"You leave immediately."

He laughed, the sound rumbling through her in a way that was altogether too pleasant. "Nice try, Kenzie. Heads, I win, tails, you lose."

She shrugged. "It was worth a shot."

He smiled slowly, and every instinct she had screamed that this was a mistake. She ignored them all. Liam dropped his arms and moved back to his seat, looking altogether too pleased with himself. "You lose, I get a kiss."

"A kiss." As if *that* wasn't suspicious. "What if I don't feel like kissing you?"

"What if I don't feel like leaving the island?"

She waved that away. "Fine, fine. Okay. One hand of blackjack. That's it."

"I'll deal."

Damn it, he really *was* onto her. She pressed a hand to her chest and affected an innocent expression. "It's almost as if you don't trust me."

"It's almost as if you cheat."

"Never!" Only when it mattered—which was every single time she bet on something worth winning. She eyed him. His being smart shouldn't make him sexier. It really wasn't fair. "How am I supposed to know if you can count cards?"

"Won't work off a single hand."

That all depended on the cards, and he'd just about admitted that he *could* count cards. She made a mental note to ban him from their blackjack tables and gave a put-upon sigh. "Poker it is." She walked past him to poke her head out the door and flag down one of the staff. A few minutes later, she had a stack of chips and a sealed deck of cards. "Texas Hold 'Em."

"Naturally." Something like amusement pulled at the edges of his lips. "I'd apologize for not playing right into your hands, but I have my own goals."

"Ask me how much I care."

This time, he did grin. "Is it any wonder I tracked you down?"

Damn it, she was flirting with him. She wasn't supposed to be flirting with him. Kenzie glanced at the camera situated in the corner of the room. She'd be hearing about this when she got back to the hub.

She shuffled a few times while Liam examined the chips and passed half to her. She'd specifically kept the amount low because this game had to end fast so she could move on to more important things.

Sure, Kenzie, that's why you're playing poker, *instead of a single hand of blackjack.*

She ignored the little voice inside and dealt each of them two cards. A quick glance at hers had her fighting down a smile. A suited ace and king. She had this in the bag. She idly tossed out two chips. "Let's make this interesting."

"If you want to make it interesting, you can start betting for clothing."

15

She wrinkled her nose. "You graduated college too long ago to think that's a clever move." And Kenzie had never gone to college in the first place. Her education was significantly more…informal. "Here on the Island of Ys, if we want to make a poker game interesting, we start betting sexual favors."

He raised his eyebrows and matched her bet. "I stand corrected."

She really needed to learn how to keep her mouth shut. Someday, over the rainbow, maybe she'd even manage it. Kenzie flipped over the three flop cards. A three, a four, and a king. It left her with a pair of kings and an ace kicker. *Yeah, I have this in the bag.*

Kenzie pretended to consider the table for a few moments and even gave her bottom lip a nibble as if she didn't know what she wanted to do. Finally, she sighed and pushed half her chips into the middle.

Liam raised his brows. "Call."

Even though she knew better, she couldn't help talking the very smallest amount of shit. "You should just bow out now and save it for the next hand. I have you beat, baby."

His only response was that small smile.

It irritated her that she couldn't distract him, that he seemed to see right through her. Kenzie flipped over the turn card and nearly crowed with victory. An ace, which meant she had two pair—and the highest on the board. It was possible Liam had good cards, but the probability of him having either two aces or two kings was astronomical. If he had an identical hand to hers, they'd split the pot and she'd be no worse off than she already was.

Kenzie gave him a sugary sweet smile. "I'm all in, baby."

Liam studied her face for a few moments. "Call." He pushed his chips in without blinking.

What the hell?

She flipped over her cards and her eyes nearly popped out of her head when he did the same. "You... You called me with a pair of threes. Do you not understand how to play this game? Because you're so bad, you're in danger of making me feel guilty, and I make it a habit never to feel guilty."

His calm expression didn't slip. "Let's see the river card before you start your victory dance."

"More like a going away party dance," she muttered. She flipped the final card over.

And stared.

"You son of a bitch."

"My mother isn't a nice lady, but I have better manners than to call her a bitch."

She blinked and then blinked again. The river card was a three. A fucking *three*. His three of a kind beat her two pair. "Shit."

"I'll be taking my kiss now." He pushed slowly to his feet. "Unless you plan on reneging on the bet.

"Never." She slowly stood. It was one kiss. She could do one kiss without losing control. Easy peasy. "This isn't going to go how you want it to," she said for the second time, trying to prove her point. Kenzie rounded the table slowly, silently debating on how to do this. Should she give him a peck and then bolt?

She stopped a few inches away, still undecided.

"Maybe." He shrugged, seeming somehow closer though she could swear he didn't move. Or maybe she was the one moving, that gravity pulling her in his direction again. Kenzie pressed her hands against his chest, having every intention of using the leverage to take a tiny kiss and shove away, but the thought went up in smoke the second she touched him. The tailored shirt was meant to downplay his body, his danger, but her hands told her the truth. Muscles pressed against her palms with each inhale he took.

17

He could break her in half.

He could try...

And, just like that, the memories of the night broke free of the safe little box where she'd shoved them. No glimpses this time, but a full montage of his hands bruising her hips as she rode his cock, as he told her how beautiful she was, as they both said things people have no business saying after knowing each other a few hours.

I wish...

If only...

Drawn by the memory haunting her, she kissed him in the here and now. It should have been cautious and testing, but Kenzie had never been cautious a single day in her life. She claimed his mouth, forcing him to meet her at the line or yield now.

Liam, damn him, met her halfway.

He hooked the back of her legs and lifted her onto the table and then stepped between the thighs she spread in welcome. This was a mistake, but she couldn't bring herself to care. Not with his hands digging into her hair, tilting her face back to give him a better angle. He tasted like whiskey, and she couldn't tell if he'd been drinking or if this was just Liam. In the end, it didn't matter. She allowed herself to drink deep of everything he offered, to throw away that last bit of control clinging stubbornly to her.

Just once.

Just once more and then I'll stop.

Just to prove it wasn't nearly as good as I remember.

Lies.

All lies.

She didn't care.

Kenzie reached down and palmed him through his slacks. Her body clenched as the feel of his cock against her hand.

Want. Need. Desire. A heady bolt of lust straight through her. She tore her mouth from his. "Liam—"

"Not yet. You kissed me. Doesn't count."

"You're not honoring the spirit of the deal." But she didn't stop him as he moved down her body, his knees hitting the floor hard enough that she heard the impact. Kenzie looked down her body at him as he shoved her dress up around her hips and used his broad shoulders to spread her legs farther. His gaze went molten. "No panties, Kenzie?"

She should rebuke him for using her name again, but how was she supposed to remember that with him practically growling the syllables straight against her pussy? He wasn't touching her, but that didn't seem to make a difference.

He glanced at her face just once, looking for some kind of confirmation that she wanted this. She could have laughed if she had the breath. She didn't want this. She fucking *needed* this. "You won, Liam. Kiss me."

"As the lady wishes." He wedged his hands under her ass and lifted her off the table to meet his mouth. She couldn't stop the sob that erupted from her as his breath caressed her clit, couldn't stop her hands from digging into his hair as he dragged his mouth over her, inhaling deeply. Savoring.

Oh god, I am in so much trouble.

* * *

LIAM HADN'T WALKED into this room with the intention of tongue fucking Kenzie, but he'd damn well do what it took to make her hold still long enough to *talk* to him.

Except they weren't talking right now.

Not with her ragged breathing filling the room and her grinding her pussy against his face as if she couldn't get enough. Christ, but he couldn't get enough either. Even when she'd driven him to the edge, he meant to maintain some semblance of control, to be the one guiding this interaction. He was a goddamn fool.

There was no controlling this.

No guiding.

They were off the rails and there was nothing as simple as common sense to pull them back.

He sucked her clit into his mouth, working her with his lips. He fucking loved the way she rolled her hips to meet him and dug her fingers into his hair, unabashedly holding his face against her pussy.

As if there was anywhere else Liam would rather be.

He shifted enough to drive two fingers into her, cursing at the way she clamped around him. "I want to fuck you, Kenzie."

"Do it." She laughed, wild and free and absolutely delighted. "Or maybe I'm going to fuck you." She tugged hard on his hair. "Put your money where your mouth is."

Liam ignored her and kept pumping his fingers into her, kept working her clit with lips and tongue. He needed to feel her come first. To have her lose control. To just once lose that goddamn smirk she wore every time she looked at him, as if he wasn't in on the joke. He wanted the *real* Kenzie, even if Liam didn't know who the fuck that was.

He'd thought he'd known once. A long time ago.

Her fingers spasmed in his hair and she came with a cry that sounded like victory. Liam wasn't done, though. He stood and undid his pants. Thank Christ he'd stashed a condom in his pocket on a whim earlier. Hope sprang eternal and all that. He rolled it onto his cock, never taking his eyes off her face. "Say yes, Kenzie."

"Mmm." She fisted his cock and gave him a rough stroke. "Yes."

Liam yanked her to the edge of the table and wasted no time notching his cock at her entrance. He had every intention of going slow, of teasing her until she went wild around him again.

The road to hell was paved with good intentions.

He slammed into her. Too rough. Too fucking rough. Liam forced himself still. "Shit, I'm sorry. Did I hurt you?"

Kenzie gripped the back of his neck, her nails digging into his skin and sending pinpricks of pain that only made the feeling of his cock buried in her pussy better. "Don't. You. Dare. Stop." She captured his bottom lip and sucked hard, making a sound like she loved the taste of herself on his mouth. "Fuck me. Hard and rough and just how I like it."

He did as she commanded. He couldn't stop himself. Each rough stroke had her breasts dangerously close to bouncing right out of that fucking tease of a dress. Each time he withdrew, she made a sound like she couldn't stand even that much distance between them.

Again, and again, and again.

Liam bent his knees and changed his angle, looking for that spot that would drive her wild. He was too close to losing himself completely, and he needed her right there on the edge with him. She reached between them to stroke her clit, taking her pleasure with ruthless abandon. Her lips parted and her head dropped back, leaving the long line of her neck that practically begged for his mouth.

He never got the chance.

Kenzie orgasmed. She locked her ankles at the small of his back and drove him deeper inside her as she came. Liam cursed, but it was too late. He followed her over the edge, helplessly driving into her again and again as he came. *Holy fuck.*

Apparently the world hadn't shifted on its axis for her, though.

She pressed a laughing kiss to his temple and gave him a gentle shove. "Off."

Off.

That was her response to this?

Liam stumbled back a few steps and went through the motions of putting himself back together. He couldn't take his eyes off her, couldn't stop himself from memorizing every detail of this moment. Even though he braced for it, her first words still drove a stake right into his chest.

"This can't mean anything."

Liam exhaled slowly. He knew as well as anyone that sex ultimately didn't shift the world on its axis for most people. Eight years past and he still hadn't put his world to rights, but Kenzie obviously had her reasons for fighting him on this. *Or she didn't feel the same way.* No, damn it, he couldn't afford to think like that. Not when she'd practically climbed him like a tree and demanded his cock. She wanted him, too. He just needed patience getting her to admit it.

Something he wouldn't be able to accomplish if he allowed himself to be shuttled off the island.

Liam watched her hop off the table and set about putting her dress to rights. He mourned every inch of skin covered and the barriers it represented, but forced himself to focus on the coming fight instead of the fact that he could still taste her on his tongue.

She would expect him to demand they talk again, so he went with a different tactic. "What happened to the woman who sponsored the guy who won the Wild Hunt? What was his name? Dolph?"

Kenzie froze in the middle of adjusting her sky-high heels. "What?"

Didn't expect that, did you?

When he first got back onto the island, he'd been too wrapped up in the loss to think about much else. Too wrapped up in the fact that the Horsemen had staged the win. It took days for the bruise on his throat to heal from where little Princess Camilla Fitzcharles had punched him there. He shook his head and put that frustration aside. It wouldn't serve him now. "The sponsor didn't leave the island, and I haven't seen her since the night she arrived. Haven't see Dolph, either."

"Surely you're not tracking every person who comes and goes from the island." She kept her voice slightly mocking, but she couldn't hide the way tension coiled through her body.

"I don't have to. All the competitors left, and there haven't been many people arriving. Makes it easy to keep track of them."

Kenzie stared. "Maybe it's the off season," she murmured.

"You didn't answer my question."

That shook her out of it. She smoothed her hands over the fabric of her dress. "I don't keep track of everyone on the island, Liam. People are free to move around as they please. Maybe she's over at Pain enjoying one of the play rooms or maybe she booked a private villa on the other side of the island. Or maybe she left, and you just didn't notice. There are a dozen places she could be that aren't directly in your line of sight. You're grasping at straws."

That confirmed what he suspected—they had rigged the game for some larger purpose. He'd never heard of the Wild Hunt before last year. He'd exhausted the resources Aiden had in searching for Kenzie, and Liam had been forced to ask Dmitri Romanov for a favor. It cost him dearly, but the Russian secured his entry in the Wild Hunt and brought him to the Island of Ys. In preparation, Liam had done his research on the past hunts. War—Kenzie—was the prey in every one of them, and she won every single time. Best he could tell, no one had ever accused her of cheating, but that didn't mean it was the truth.

"I could help," he said softly. "I'm not without resources."

Kenzie stopped and looked at him. "What resources could you possibly offer me that I don't already have?"

It was a fair point. The Horsemen were a relatively new phenomenon—a four-person group who had risen to power rapidly ten years ago. No one knew where they'd come from or who they were aside from their monikers, but the Island of Ys had become known for the place to go to have a person's every fantasy fulfilled. There were no limits on what they provided, but it all came with a hefty price tag.

With that in mind, even split four ways, Kenzie was still richer than anyone he'd ever met, and they lived in a world where money accomplished damn near anything a person could dream of.

"Someone in your corner."

She laughed. The sound seemed to fill up the room and created a funny feeling in his chest, even though she laughed at his expense. Kenzie flicked her golden hair off her shoulder. "I have someone in my corner—three someones, to be specific. And, unlike whatever you're trying to accomplish, they *actually* have my back in every way that counts." She moved to the door. "Like I said, there's nothing you can offer me that I don't already have."

"Kenzie."

She didn't look at him. "If you use my name in public again, I'll hurt you."

"You'll try."

Now she turned to him. "No, Liam. I *will* hurt you. I might not enjoy it, but I'll do it. Leave the island. There's nothing for you here." She walked out the door without another word.

Liam sank into one of the chairs and dropped his head into his hands. That hadn't gone like he'd wanted. Fuck, none of this had gone like he planned when he first set out to find the woman who'd haunted him for so long.

He'd thought she was someone who had been down on their luck at the time, who was maybe still dancing on the wrong side of the law, but who he could approach in a normal way and get to know better to see if things were worth pursuing.

What he'd got instead was War.

CHAPTER 3

"*S*ubtle as always."

Kenzie slammed into the chair next to Ryu and crossed her arms over her chest. "Bite me. He's wily. He won't listen to reason."

Ryu shook his head, his dark gaze never straying from the monitors that covered a full wall in the hub where they kept their personal rooms. He and Amarante were the only two of their little family that actually shared blood, both harkening from a well-to-do family in China before they were stolen from their beds in the middle of the night. Of the four of them, Kenzie was the only one who had no real history, who couldn't have returned to her family even if she wanted to. The other three had chosen to keep ties cut after they fought their way to freedom.

Kenzie had no choice.

Dark thoughts, but these were dark times.

She cleared her throat. "Have you tracked down the people behind the names yet?"

Ryu cut her a look. "That change of subject was blunt, even for you. You know you can't avoid this forever."

"I can't even avoid this for the next twelve hours. Throw me a bone here, Ryu. I need something to focus on while I figure out my next step." She *knew* how ludicrous she sounded. There would be no *next step* required if she'd just done the job of getting Liam off the island to begin with. She'd never pulled her punches or shied away from doing distasteful tasks that buoyed their bottom line before. There was absolutely no reason to do it now.

Liar, liar, pants on fire.

Ryu finally shook his head. "This is what I have." A few flicks of his fingers on the keyboard and three of the monitors changed to show dossiers. Kenzie pushed to her feet to get a closer look. She frowned at the first one. "I know this guy."

"He's been on the island quarterly since we opened it." Another few clicks and the monitor next to the dossier showed one of the profiles they kept on every guest who came there. Likes, dislikes, ties to various power structures. Declan MacAllister," she read aloud. "Yeah, that's the guy who's into pony play and high-stakes blackjack."

"The very same."

She'd *talked* to him before, had smiled at him. All while not knowing he'd been a key part of the nightmare she shared with her siblings. But then, how could she have known? Five years in that hellhole and every one of her tormentors had worn masks. Oh, she could use other things to identify them, but nothing about Declan had ever rang any bells. Not his voice, the way he moved, his attitude. Nothing. "He's not one of mine."

"No, he handled security, both of the kids and of the visitors."

She shuddered and then cursed herself for showing that much reaction. It wasn't her fault. Kenzie needed to blow off steam regularly and, what was more, she counted on the seven days of the annual Wild Hunt to purge herself of the dark thoughts that clung to her during the rest of the year. When she was out in the jungle that covered the big island, outwitting the competitors and surviving on wiles and sheer skill... That was the only time she felt truly whole.

And she hadn't been able to do it this year because Amarante was determined to prove a point by making an example of the princess.

Focus, Kenzie.

She glanced at Ryu. "So we wait until he comes here and we nab him just like we nabbed the Bookkeeper?"

"I suspect that will be the plan."

"Good." If he somehow caught wind that they were onto him, they could adapt the plan as necessary. She moved on to the next one. Arthur Perez. He had the look of a thousand other Spanish men, totally nondescript in a way designed to fly below the radar. "Acquisitions," she read. "This is the fucker responsible for taking us."

"Not him alone. I suspect at least half the kids in that place were sold."

Was I?

She already knew Luca had been stolen. His family—his *country*—had moved heaven and earth to find him, and then to try and bring him back into the fold once they did. Too little, too late, but Kenzie was self-aware enough to recognize the sliver of jealousy in her heart of hearts. The Horsemen were her family now, no matter where she'd come from, but it still would have been a little nice to know that she was wanted.

She glanced at the final dossier and flinched. "I know this one."

"Yes," Ryu said quietly.

Not the face. She'd never seen his face since all the enemy wore masks. But the rose tattoo on his neck? She knew every detail of that tattoo, had spent hours innumerable imagining driving a knife right through it. "He's mine."

"That's not a good idea."

With her history of impulse control? Yeah, it wasn't a good idea in the least. She didn't care. "He's mine," she repeated. "We all have our own vengeance to deal out. This one is for me."

"There's the bottom line to consider..." He held up his hands when she turned on him. "Take it up with Amarante. She's putting together the next step."

That seemed to imply that she hadn't known the next step before they put any of this into place. Some days Kenzie was sure Amarante had her vengeance and fury mapped out before they ever obtained their freedom. She was always the most forward looking of them, which was why they cleaved to her. "Where is she?"

"Her room."

No reason to put this off, then. Kenzie nodded and strode to the north hall leading from the hub. Each of their suites were identical in layout, if not in decoration. They'd built Pleasure with the hub and their rooms at the center, as well as a warren of halls and rooms inside the main casino gambling hall designed to trick the senses and hide the fact that a good portion of space was unaccounted for publicly in the center of the building.

She knocked on Amarante's door and walked through a few seconds later. The other woman sat at her desk, typing at her computer. She paused to hold a single finger up and then went back to whatever she was working on.

Kenzie knew better than to interrupt her, so she perched on the arm of the small couch and studied her sister while she waited. Amarante wore suits better than most men did, all of them tailored to perfection. Today it was black pinstriped slacks and vest with a vivid green button up. She even had diamond cufflinks.

She finally sat back and turned her chair to face Kenzie. "Is he gone?"

"Not yet."

Amarante raised a single dark brow. "I'm not one to question your methods, but perhaps you can explain how hooking up with him in that conference room was supposed to convince him to leave."

Damn Ryu for tattling. She examined her red-painted nails. "Ryu needs to get a hobby."

Amarante didn't blink. "And you need to get control of yourself. Would you rather I take care of it?"

"No." She said the word too forcefully, a blatant tell.

Amarante sighed. "I'm honestly curious, Kenzie. Because it looks like you lost your head at the worst possible time. We need you focused."

She knew that. Obviously, she knew that. "I won't compromise the plan."

"You're distracted. *He's* distracting you."

She couldn't even argue. It was the truth. Even when she didn't have a direct line of sight on Liam, she could feel his presence on the island, a pulse through her body that was nearly impossible to ignore. It didn't matter that it was all in her imagination. "I'll take care of it."

Amarante looked like she wanted to argue further, but she finally nodded. "Ryu has tracked the three names the Bookkeeper gave us."

"Yeah, he updated me."

"Good." She leaned forward. "We have to take them all at once."

Kenzie gratefully switched from thinking about Liam to thinking about vengeance. The plan they had in place was so much simpler than the conflicting emotions churning in her chest. "Keep it quick and clean and ensure word doesn't get out."

"Word will get out." Amarante gave a thin smile. "Even people like this don't disappear without someone taking notice. It's a matter of controlling the flow of information."

There was also the fact that people were a whole lot easier to snatch if they didn't know they were in danger in the first place. "I want Neck Tattoo."

Amarante tilted her head to the side, her long black hair shining in the low light. "Do you think that's wise?"

"I don't care if it's wise. It's what I need to do."

"He has to be brought in alive, Kenzie. He's no use to us dead—not yet."

She bit back a sharp reply. Bickering with Amarante never did any good, and she needed her sister to take her seriously this once. "I can handle it."

Finally, she nodded. "Okay. We move the second Declan arrives on the island. You'll take that one and Luca will handle Arthur."

That got her attention. "You're asking me if I can handle it. Why aren't you asking *him?* Luca's the one all wrapped up in that princess." Her words tasted bitter, but she couldn't help it. She was happy for Luca, in a way. He'd found something she was convinced didn't exist. A person who saw the truth of him and didn't flinch. A woman who loved him and was strong enough to stand at his side.

She was also self-aware enough to realize she was a little jealous.

Okay, a lot jealous.

Seems like I am forever jealous of my siblings..

"We accept this, or we lose him." Amarante said it so calmly, as if it was just that easy. Maybe for her it was. She tended to see the world in black or white—in things that served her end game or didn't. She saw family the same way.

31

They were family, so she protected them and did what it took to ensure they were safe. Kenzie had always been under the impression that happiness never entered into the equation.

No, that wasn't fair. Amarante's responsibilities didn't include ensuring they were all happy and content. She promised safety and vengeance. That's what fused them together into a family unit when they were traumatized children just trying to survive. That's what kept them going as teenagers trying to claw their way up in the world.

Amarante was the driving force that led them to this island and helped build this world from the ground up.

As a result, it was exactly that simple to her. They accepted Luca's lady love, or they ran the risk of him walking away from them the same way he turned his back on his first family after they failed to protect him as a child.

"Kenzie," Amarante's voice cut through her whirling thoughts. "Is this going to be a problem? Any of this?"

"No, of course not." She gave a practiced smile, shoving her turmoil down deep, locking it away. It served no purpose and so it wasn't worth experiencing. "When can we expect Declan?"

Her sister's gaze missed nothing. "He has a standing reservation two weeks from now. We have to keep up appearances that everything is functioning as normal until then. No waves. No drama beyond the expected stuff that crops up with guests. No distractions."

No Liam was what she meant.

"I'll take care of it."

"Kenzie."

She froze in the middle of turning away. "Yeah?"

"Would it help or hurt to get him out of your system now?"

Damn Amarante for even offering her this option. But

32

then, her sister always did see right to the very heart of her. Kenzie wanted to say that she didn't need that kind of reckless action, that she could hold to the plan without stepping outside the line just this once. She wanted to...but she couldn't. "I don't know."

"Do what you have to do. Just make sure he's gone before Declan gets here."

If she was a better person, her heart wouldn't race with anticipation. If she had more control like Ryu, or was cold like Amarante, she wouldn't need to act out like this. To make brazen mistakes that hurt her as much as they hurt the people around her.

But she'd never hurt the plan.

She nodded. "He'll be off the island by then. I promise."

"Then go and have your fun." Again that fleeting smile. "One of us should."

Because Amarante didn't sleep with anyone ever. Well, there was one exception, but everything around it had been so hush-hush, Kenzie still wasn't sure of the details. Her sister wasn't exactly the biggest sharer in the world. And Ryu was a control freak of the highest order. He didn't like to be touched, and he never imbibed in anything that would slow that impressive brain of his.

Kenzie gave her sister a wide grin. "I'll have enough fun for all three of us."

* * *

LIAM STALKED AROUND HIS ROOM, frustration boiling through him. Being with Kenzie again, being *inside* Kenzie again, should have smoothed out the worst of this thing driving him. Instead it had only made it stronger. Once wasn't enough. If it had been, he wouldn't be here, chasing her down like he was some kind of crazy person.

He rounded on the phone, but changed his mind before bothering to pick it up. He already knew what Aiden would say. *Come home. Find a nice Irish girl to settle down with. Stop chasing this phantom.* Even when he had his hands on her skin, she still felt ethereal, like she'd slip through his fingers again if given half a chance.

But then, she already told him it meant nothing.

Fuck, but he hated that.

For better or worse, Liam didn't screw around. He was no monk, but he preferred his sex to mean something. Fucking someone he didn't respect or care about... he might as well jack himself instead and save the trouble that came from involving another person.

It couldn't be clearer that Kenzie didn't feel the same way.

He let loose a harsh breath. It wasn't over. She wanted him, and that was something he could work with. He just needed *time*. Time he didn't have. At some point Death would decide to get involved, and if he could needle Kenzie until she cracked, he had no illusions about the woman known as Death.

The old saying about the female being the deadlier of the species was never truer than when it came to the Horsemen. The men—Famine and Pestilence—were both well-known because of their skillset. Famine handled all the security and enforcing it on the island. Pestilence was some kind of computer wizard who ensured that if the physical threats Famine offered weren't enough deterrent, then Pestilence's threats *were*. Liam had heard of people having everything from their bank account to their actual identities disappear after failing to hold to the rules governing the island.

He suspected Pestilence was the one behind the Horsemen's meteoric financial rise, too.

But War and Death? They were the ones that seemed to both fascinate and terrify people in turn. Death never made empty threats, and she played a deeper game he could only guess at. War? She was as loud and vibrant and dangerous as her namesake, dealing violence as easily as she breathed. She was the center of every event they hosted on the island, the more extravagant and over the top, the better. The Wild Hunt and fighting matches and more shit than he could name—she organized it all.

She participated in it all.

So reckless. So fucking *reckless* of her to throw her life on the line time and time again for…what? They were established enough now that they didn't need the draw she offered so regularly. She didn't need to fight and bloody herself.

Which meant she wanted to do it.

This was crazy. What was he doing? Everyone told him he had no idea what he was walking into, but he'd ignored them because he knew in his gut that it was the right call to make. That surety that had carried him through months of frustration and five days in hell during the Wild Hunt faltered now.

If she banished him from the island…

Well, that would be a clear line in the sand. Liam was many things, but he didn't make a habit of pursuing women that wanted nothing to do with him. That's what Kenzie claimed she wanted—nothing to do with him.

Then why the hell had she had sex with him in that boardroom?

He ran his hands through his hair, cursing so hard he almost missed the knock on his door. Liam stalked down the hall and threw it open. Despite everything, his breath caught at the sight of her. She'd changed in the hours since he'd seen her last, now wearing a short black dress that dipped low between her breasts and tights with a pattern of thorns and roses winding up her legs. Her long blond hair was pulled back into a complicated style that he wanted to run his fingers through. Fuck, he was losing his mind.

Kenzie cocked her hip out and grinned. "So, funny story."

"I'm all ears."

She tsked. "I'm bored out of my mind, and you're here. I have a proposal."

Liam blinked. Blinked again. Surely she didn't say what he thought she just said. He held up a hand. "I'm not a toy, Kenzie."

"We've talked about what I'll do to you if you keep using that name."

"And we've talked about how much I don't give a fuck." He looked around, but she was alone in the hall. Liam finally stepped back and allowed her to walk past him into his rooms. He shut the door and followed her, watching her as she poked around the stuff he had scattered around. "You said you have a proposal."

"I do." She leaned over to run her fingers along a shirt he'd laid out, giving him an impressive view of her ass. Kenzie wasn't one of those tiny, breakable women with bird bones. She was an athlete and it showed in the shape of her legs and arms, the lines of her exposed back, and the curve of her ass.

He looked away, but the temptation of watching her in close quarters was too strong to deny. Liam finally dropped into a chair and let her snoop. She rifled through the clothes he'd hung in the closet, poked at the pages he'd printed out for research and the laptop he had set up on the desk, and finally dug through the small fridge, coming up with two beers. She grinned. "Okay, so it goes like this. You still have to leave."

"You've said that before."

She ignored him. "But I can be persuaded to fudge the timeline a little."

It wasn't what he wanted, but it was more than he'd expected. Liam already knew her well enough to know there was a catch involved. "I'm listening."

"So stoic. It's both frustrating and sexy." She passed him one of the beers and perched on the edge of the bed. "I propose a friendly little wager."

"Pass."

She blinked those big hazel eyes at him, the very picture of innocence. The little liar. "Excuse me?"

"We tried that before. I won. You lost."

"Last time. Next time is not last time."

That's what he was afraid of. "I'm not wagering with you. You cheat."

"That's a horrible allegation."

"It's a fact."

Kenzie looked like she considered arguing and finally waved it away. "The conditions go like this—you beat me, and you get me for a week. Seven days, no more." She took a slow pull off her beer, her cherry red lips wrapping around the bottle.

Jesus.

"And when I win, you leave immediately. No arguments, no second chances. You're gone and that's that."

Liam shook his head, trying to focus. "A week isn't good enough."

"Excuse the hell out of me, you couldn't survive more than a week with me. Those are generous terms and you're not going to get better." She crossed her legs. "The alternative, of course, is that I call my brothers and they haul your ass off the island here and now."

"Famine isn't even in the same hemisphere right now."

Her eyes flashed. "He'll be back."

It seemed to be a sore point, so he let it go. "What's the wager?"

"I knew I had your attention."

What she had was him over a barrel. Liam was out of options. Winning this wager, whatever it was, would buy him more time. A priceless commodity, especially when he still couldn't get a read on this Kenzie versus the one he'd spent a night with eight years ago. People changed—he knew that better than anyone—and one night was hardly enough time to know a person completely. Normally. But he knew in his heart of hearts that they'd made the kind of connection he'd lived his entire life craving.

If that wasn't worth fighting for, what was?

"I'm listening."

CHAPTER 4

$\mathscr{L}$iam turned and looked at the arena for the third time. It wasn't a large one as such things went, but it was still *a fucking arena*. An arena empty of people, but that didn't change the presence of a boxing ring in the middle of the floor space. Because why the hell not?

When Kenzie had said they'd wager, he'd been under the impression that she meant over cards again. Or something of that nature.

Not a full out brawl for victory.

Liam worked his ass off to be prepared for any challenge that arose, and in his line of work that often meant preparing for violence. Even in peacetime, the O'Malleys had their share of small conflicts, and he kept himself in fighting shape. That should have given him an edge in this competition.

He knew better.

Kenzie wanted to fight him. In a fair fight, he was reasonably confident that he could take her. He had a longer reach and even if she was trained—and she was—he also had her on strength and height. There was one key problem.

He didn't want to hurt her.

That desire would hold him back, would slow him down, and it would give her an edge he wasn't sure he could match. His best bet was to get her on the ground and force her to tap out, but knowing what he did of the woman, nothing short of true defeat would work. He'd *have* to hurt her.

Fuck.

Liam took a breath and tried to push down the sudden queasy feeling in his stomach. So much rode on this. So fucking much.

Kenzie walked through the large doors on the other side of the arena like she owned the place. She wore a pair of tiny shorts and a sports bra, and for the first time since he'd come here, she didn't have on the sky-high heels. Instead, she was barefoot. Even from this distance, Liam could see that her toenails were painted a pretty pink and something in him went tight in response.

She wasn't alone. A man and a woman, both Asian, stood at her back. Death and Pestilence. He wasn't sure if they were there to stand at witness or to ensure Liam lost, but he couldn't afford to let it worry him.

I can't lose.

Kenzie sashayed down the steps and up to toward the ring, talking in that voice designed to project to Liam's position without her having to yell. "The rules are simple. First one to tap out or be knocked out loses. Simple."

"You're crazy if you think I'm knocking you out."

The mask didn't quite drop from her face, but it dimmed a little. "Baby, I wasn't talking about my being knocked out. I was talking about *you*. Get ready to see some cute birdies flying around that giant head of yours."

"You have a high opinion of yourself."

Kenzie laughed, the sound loud and free and completely

unencumbered. "Of course I do. Wouldn't you if you were me?"

He couldn't argue that, so he didn't bother. Liam eyed the ring, hating what came next. He wore basketball shorts that were probably too loose for this sort of thing, but he'd make it work. The shirt had to go, though. He pulled it over his head and dropped it on top of his shoes.

Which was right around the time he noticed Kenzie staring. Pure satisfaction surged. No matter how much she liked to play at nonchalance, being around him affected her. They wouldn't be going through this song and dance if he didn't. He knew that.

Seeing it was something else entirely.

Her gaze was stuck on his chest and as he watched, she bit her bottom lip the same way she had when he was inside here earlier today. He could use this. She'd been playing dirty since they met, and Liam didn't have a chance in hell of winning this wager unless he sank to her level.

He stalked closer to her, and she finally managed to jerk her eyes to his face when he stood a few inches away. He didn't stop, though. Liam took that last step, bringing them chest to chest, and dipped down to claim her mouth as if he'd already won.

It took everything he had not to sink into the taste of her, to work her up even as he fought for control within himself. Only went she went soft against him did he lift his head and step back, leaving her weaving on her feet. "Good luck, Kenzie."

She lifted a slightly shaking hand to press to her lips. "Playing dirty."

"Using the tools at my disposal."

Suddenly, she laughed. "I can't even be mad about it." She spun to face the Death and Pestilence where they'd taken front seats next to the ring.

Now wasn't the time for doubts or hesitation. If he blinked, Kenzie would kick his ass.

He took a slow breath, pushing the whirling thoughts in his head to the side. They'd still be there at the end of this, but he might not be if he couldn't focus. It was the same process he went through before walking into danger for Aiden over the years. He wasn't likely to get shot in this arena, but the same principle applied.

Another breath and then a buzzer went off and there was no more time for anything but the fight.

Kenzie came at him like a tornado. She was even faster than he'd anticipated, striking with punches it took everything he had to deflect. Damn it, how was he going to pull this off? He jabbed at her, but she swatted his strike away.

And then she tried to kick him in the balls.

Liam twisted his hips at last moment, taking the blow in the thigh. "What the fuck?"

Her infectious laugh was her only response.

When he won this thing, he was going to put her over his knee and paddle her ass. He threw himself at her, sheer fury ensuring he barely registered her punches. A distant part of him knew he'd feel the bruises later. *She* wasn't worried about hurting him.

He tackled her around the waist and took them to the ground. Liam got his arm out to break their fall, so she didn't take the full brunt of his weight, and then he instantly had to change tactics when she tried to headbutt him.

This wouldn't work. He could pin her down all day, but she'd keep fighting him until the end of time. Liam cursed and moved, using his superior strength to force her into an arm bar. Kenzie whimpered in pain, but he didn't let up. "That weepy performance won't work on me."

She tensed. "So cold, Liam. Tsk, tsk." Her voice was only slightly rough from pain.

He readjusted his grip on her wrist. "Tap out or I break it."

"You wouldn't dare."

"Anything to win, Kenzie. *Anything.*"

She hesitated, clearly weighing her options, and he wrenched her arm back a little farther. Finally, Kenzie cursed and slapped the mat. Liam didn't hesitate. He surged to his feet and grabbed her, and tossed her over his shoulder.

Kenzie smacked his back. "Hey!"

No way was he putting her down. If he did, she'd just find some other caveat or loophole to save face in front of Death and Pestilence. He pointed his free hand at them. "You saw her tap out."

Death raised an eyebrow and Pestilence shrugged as if bored by the whole show. Well, fuck him. He could be bored as long as he didn't challenge Liam's win. When it became apparent that neither of them would, he climbed out of the ring and strode up the same way Kenzie had entered the arena. He just needed somewhere quiet that he could stop and *think*. Where he could talk to Kenzie.

The walkway led into a large room that held more shit than he'd ever seen in his life. It looked like a combination of behind the scenes at a Broadway show and an MMA locker room. He moved to a large crate that held god knew what and set Kenzie on it. Liam took a quick step back, half expecting her to strike, but she just set about fixing her hair.

She looked...calm.

Alarms blazed through him. A dramatic Kenzie he could deal with. He didn't trust this buttoned up version of her. He didn't trust it one bit. "You tried to kick me in the balls."

"And?" She finished with her hair and propped her hands on the crate behind her. The position arched her back a little and gave the impression she offered her breasts to him. They were amazing breasts, large enough that they wouldn't fit his hands.

Liam allowed himself to drink in the sight of her. The lean lines of muscles pressing against her skin representing unknown hours of hard work, the softness of her stomach that said she enjoyed life, and those pink, pink toes.

He scrubbed a hand over his face. "I won."

"Yep." Kenzie grinned. "You've got me for seven days. That's almost one for every year since I robbed you. I bet you can dream up any number of punishments."

Damn it, but he didn't want to *punish* her. That wasn't what this was about, and she knew it. She had to know it.

The woman made him want to rip his hair out in frustration. "Kenzie—"

"That's about enough talking, don't you think?" She hopped off the crate and then she was pressed against him, soft and hot and sliding her hands up his bare chest to loop her arms around his neck. Kenzie kissed him before he could say anything.

He should stop this. He wanted to talk to her, to get to know her better, to spend some time with her in an interaction that wasn't a straight up confrontation.

Liam didn't stop it.

The pull of her was simply too strong. He dug his fingers into her hair and lost himself in the taste of her. Kenzie was more intoxicating than any whiskey he'd ever drank. And just as likely to set him on his ass.

She broke the kiss and backed up a step. "I don't want to wait anymore." She pulled her bra over her head and shimmied out of her shorts.

His breath stalled in his lungs. Clothed, she reminded him of those Amazonian tree frogs, the ones that were bright and beautiful and completely deadly. Naked… Naked, she was so much more dangerous. "Anyone could walk in."

"That's part of the fun." She leaned back against the crate, her hazel eyes full of challenge. "If you have performance anxiety…"

"Christ, Kenzie." He took a step toward her and stopped. "What I don't have is a condom."

"Oh, that." She waved it away as if it wasn't the least bit of a problem. "I'm on this nifty invention called birth control. And while I'm hardly celibate, I am very, very careful and get tested regularly."

He wanted to fuck her bare. He really, really did. But if he let her set the tone of this now, he'd never regain the upper hand. They didn't have enough trust between them for this conversation. Not yet.

Liam stalked to her and yanked her off the crate. He spun her around and planted her hands on the wood. "Don't move."

"That's not really my—"

He pressed himself to her, covering every inch of the back of her body with his. Liam bracketed her throat with one hand and slid his other down her stomach to cup her pussy. "You think you're in charge. You're not." Her breath hitched and he felt that little response down to his very soul. He spoke directly in her ear, soft and steady despite his body practically shaking with the need to drive into her. To fuck her until they both forgot why they were fighting in the first place.

Not yet.

Liam dragged his mouth along her neck. "If I do something you don't like, you tell me, but you don't get to give orders. Not with me. Not for the next seven days." A single week to convince her… What?

He'd worry about that particular detail later.

"Do you understand?"

She pushed back against him, but he held her mostly

45

immobile. Kenzie cursed. "Fine. You win. I understand." She rolled her hips, but he wouldn't give her what she wanted. Liam kept his hand tight against her, denying her the friction she obviously craved. "Where's your room?"

"Fuck that. We're not going to my room. We're going to yours."

He considered pushing the issue, but decided this wasn't the hill to die on. She'd conceded one thing. It would be enough to start. He took a breath, inhaling the citrusy scent of her.

Liam released her and stepped back. "Get dressed."

"Excuse me."

"You heard me."

Kenzie snatched up her discarded clothes and yanked them on, glaring at him all the while. "I don't like you very much right now."

"You didn't like me very much to begin with." Another area to conquer, another thing to think about later. Facing her down, Liam threw his initial plan out the window. He wouldn't be able to talk to her, not like this. She'd fight him every step of the way, and in seven days she'd kick his ass off the island with glee.

No, the only way forward was to fuck Kenzie into submission. To foster an addiction for what only he could provide. To make her need him enough that she wouldn't banish him.

That plan began now.

CHAPTER 5

*K*enzie had miscalculated. She had planned on losing, sure, but on her terms. Liam surprised her with the tackle, and then he surprised her again when he wouldn't follow through on the lust sparking between them. Lust, she could deal with.

Lust, she embraced fully.

She'd thought to control him. He was only a man, after all, and most men were content to be led around by their dicks as long as their other needs were met and no one rocked the boat too much. Or that was Kenzie's theory. No way to really know since she didn't do relationships. How could she when so much of her life was wrapped up in the island and her siblings? There was no time or energy to try to get to know someone more than the shared drink it took to seduce them. Even when the hook ups lasted days or even a week or two, it stayed very firmly in the physical realm. Her partners weren't interested in Kenzie for her conversational skills, and while she might be comfortable sharing her body, she refused to do anything to endanger her heart.

Was it kind of lonely? Sure. But everything had its price,

and this one she was willing to pay. Whenever it got too overwhelming, she either went into the ring to burn off some energy, or she closeted herself in her room and read the romance novels she wouldn't admit to owning. It was nice to believe that there were normal people out there who didn't suffer from the kind of trauma that burned away any chance of a real world happily ever after.

Besides, relationships took trust.

Kenzie didn't trust anyone except her siblings.

Liam stopped in front of his door and unlocked it. He didn't look at her as he held it open for her to precede him, didn't give her anything to work with. Everything about him had gone cold on the walk from the arena to the room, until he was more ice than man.

She didn't like it.

She sure as hell didn't trust it.

He locked the door behind them and then leaned against it. "Strip."

Kenzie considered arguing, but curiosity sank its teeth into her. He obviously had reached some conclusion on the walk over here, and she wanted to know what it was. She shrugged and stripped. "If you wanted me naked, you got the full show ten minutes ago."

He didn't respond other than to push off the door. She braced herself, but Liam moved past her on his way into the bathroom. Several seconds later the shower turned on.

She blinked. *Okay, then.*

"Kenzie." Her name. A command.

She obeyed without thinking, her body going on autopilot and walking her into the bathroom to join him. Liam opened the shower and pointed to it. "In."

It wasn't until she stepped beneath the spray that she realized he hadn't joined her. She turned around and saw him take a seat on the bench across from the broad glass doors. Kenzie frowned. "Voyeur."

"Exhibitionist."

Well... He wasn't wrong.

She shrugged and tilted her head back to wet her hair. Since Liam didn't seem that interested in conversation, Kenzie ignored him. Okay, that wasn't the truth. There was no ignoring his presence in the room. Not when she could feel his gaze tracing the lines of water coursing over her naked body. She wanted his hands on those lines, his mouth. What was the point of losing if she wasn't going to get the sex she so desperately wanted?

She didn't wash her hair—the products they kept in the rooms on the island were top notch, but she was picky and liked her own stuff—but she took a long time soaping up her hands and slowly running them over her body. All the while not looking at her audience. If he was going to leave her aching and wanting him, she would punish him for it.

Until he lost control and gave them what they both wanted.

Except he didn't lose control. He sat there and silently watched her and *she* was the one left shaking with need. *Damn it.* Kenzie cleared her throat. "Liam..."

"Out."

Was he going to communicate in one-word commands from now on? Where was the man who just wanted to talk to her, to convince her to... Well, she still wasn't sure what he'd wanted to convince her to do. To bang him until they tired of each other? To admit that, yes, she remembered that night and, sure, it had been really good sex and, okay fine, they had the kind of instant connection she'd only read about.

None of that mattered in the long run.

Amarante would guide Kenzie and her siblings to both

49

vengeance and justice, and that was more important than anything as short-term as attraction.

Even if it was blazing white-hot universe-ending attraction.

She stepped out of the shower and Liam engulfed her in a giant white fluffy towel. When she went to take it from him, he stilled her with a glare. She huffed out a breath. "Fine. Dry me like I'm playing the part of your own personal blow-up doll."

"I don't put my blow-up doll in the shower."

She blinked. Had he just made a joke? Nothing showed on his face, so she couldn't quite be sure but... Yeah, he definitely just made a joke.

Liam finished drying her and wrapped her up in the towel. "Sit."

"Woof."

His mouth definitely quirked that time, but she didn't get a chance to enjoy provoking a response because he chose that moment to shuck off his shorts.

Holy shit.

She should probably try to be aloof or unaffected or something, but she couldn't drag her gaze away from his naked body. She'd seen him naked before, of course, but eight years was a long time and she'd been too busy coming earlier to worry about the sight of Liam's cock. Besides, Kenzie was very good at encouraging her memory to falter when it mattered most. That skill was the only way she made it through her days intact.

Liam was tall, but held the kind of lean strength that spoke of the quick strikes and fluid dodges he'd displayed in the ring. This man was more blade than tank. Scars marked his body, and even through her foggy memory, she knew one of them hadn't been there last time. A puckered bullet wound on his chest, dangerously close to his heart.

An inch, maybe two, and he wouldn't have survived. With that kind of wound it was possible he *shouldn't* have survived.

She went cold at the thought. "Who shot you?"

"Which time?" He didn't look at her, soaping his body in smooth economical movements.

"Don't screw with me. You know which time. Who tried to kill you with a shot to your chest?"

He paused and ducked under the spray, rinsing the soap away. Liam shut the water off and turned to face her. "It doesn't matter. She's dead now. My best friend's sister killed her."

A woman after my own heart.

"How?"

He gave her a sharp look. "Does it matter?"

It shouldn't but... "Yes, it matters."

He sighed. "She shot her several times in the chest."

Kenzie nodded. "That's got some poetic justice right there, though I would have liked her to suffer more."

"You aren't the only one." With that cryptic statement, he finished drying off and pulled her to her feet. He took both their towels and neatly folded them on the bench and then pressed a hand to the small of her back and guided her into the bedroom.

Toward the bed.

She bit her bottom lip. *Finally.* The hookup in the boardroom earlier had been good, really good, but she wanted more. Needed more. "I *am* tested regularly. I know that sounds like a line—and probably the birth control bit—but I have the papers to prove it."

"Kenzie."

"Yeah?"

"Stop talking." He gave her a push that sent her flopping onto the soft mattress. She rolled onto her back and glared, but Liam didn't give her a chance to respond. He stared her down. "I'm tested regularly, too."

"Great, then—"

"Kenzie."

She shut her mouth. She couldn't remember the last time someone who wasn't her siblings said her name. It might have been Liam all those years ago. God, what had she gotten herself into?

"Do ties bother you?"

The change of subject was enough to give her whiplash and she answered more honestly than she would have otherwise. "I'd rather chew off my own arm than be tied up."

Liam nodded like he expected no less. He pointed at the top of the bed. "Lie down. Hands on the bottom of the headboard."

She inched back until she could do as he commanded. Even as part of her demanded she fight this, the rest of her was too turned on by what might come next to worry about her submission setting a dangerous precedent.

It was only seven days.

Only in the bedroom.

She reached over her head and clasped the thick wooden headboard. Its edges were rounded, seeming made to fit against the palm of her hand. "Now what?"

Liam moved around to the foot of the bed. "Spread your legs."

She didn't hesitate nearly as long this time. The way he looked at her...the promise in those dark eyes... Why fight when this was exactly what they both wanted? She even arched her back a little, giving him a show. "Touch me."

"When I'm ready." He crawled onto the bed and knelt between her spread thighs. If she moved, she could touch him, but there was something so deliciously sexy about this *almost* touch, about obeying, that she forced herself to wait.

Liam hovered his hand directly over her pussy. "Another bet."

She blinked. "What?"

"Another bet," he repeated. "Fifteen minutes. If you keep your hands there for fifteen minutes, then you get control for the next hour."

Fifteen minutes. A blink of time or a small eternity. "And if I don't?"

"Then you don't get my cock today." He fisted himself and gave a rough stroke. "Not in any way."

This was definitely a trick. It had to be. Kenzie glanced at the headboard and then back at Liam. She was *War*. She could control herself for fifteen minutes, no matter what he did to her. She'd endured literal torture, for fuck's sake, and other horrible things that she very intentionally never thought about.

Liam would never hurt her. She might not be sure of much when it came to him, but she was sure of that. What was fifteen minutes of pleasure in the face of an hour of control over this sexy man?

Kenzie grinned. "Game on, Liam. I'm going to really, really enjoy playing with you for that hour."

His gaze when white hot and he finally let his hand drop to touch her, pushing two fingers deep inside her. "We'll see, won't we?"

As he settled between her thighs, Kenzie had the sudden suspicion that she'd made a terrible mistake. She glanced at the clock. "Nine forty-three."

"Noted." He kept up those languid strokes, exploring her pussy as if he wasn't on a timer. As if he had all night for just this. "You're beautiful."

"I know."

He nodded, his expression still completely unreadable. She hadn't understood how much she relied on Liam's reactions until he took them from her. Kenzie shifted, uncomfortable with the realization.

Liam pressed his free hand against her stomach, pinning her in place as he kept up that languid stroking. "What could a woman who lives on this island possibly need that she's unable to acquire? All you have to do is crook your finger and there is a line of men willing to drop to their knees and let you ride their mouth just for the sake of needing you."

She dug her heels into the mattress, desire flaring at the picture he painted. She'd never done anything like that. There were boundaries, after all. But fuck if it didn't turn her on something fierce. "And women."

Liam didn't pause. "And women." He laughed hoarsely. "I'm a bastard and a half, because that's sexy as fuck. Just imagine…" He twisted his wrist, pressing the spot inside her that made every muscle go molten. "I'm sitting on the edge of the bed and you're riding my cock, your back to my chest." He paused. "Are you imagining it, Kenzie?"

She couldn't help but obey. He'd filled her so perfectly earlier, it was the smallest of jumps to imagine them in exactly that position. His hands on her body, his thighs forcing hers wide. "Yes," she gasped.

He began finger fucking her again, but he circled her clit with his thumb now, too. Slowly. So freaking slowly. Each stroke cutting another tether between her and the reasons she should fight this man. Liam watched her with eyes gone so dark, they were nearly black. "She'd be on her knees in the doorway. Got to work for that pussy, doesn't she? We'd make her crawl."

Oh fuck.

Kenzie couldn't stop the whimper that escaped her lips.

He never stopped touching her, but he shifted to lie next to her, his big body stretched out next to hers. It wasn't the position he'd described, but it was close enough. "I think she'd lick her lips. Who could look at you like this and not want a taste?" He ran his mouth along her shoulder the slow slide of his tongue a direct counterpoint to the rough stumble on his cheek. "I'll tell you who. Not a single fucking person. She's no different. She's wet for you, Kenzie. Desperate and needy."

She had to get control of this, had to do something to break the illusion he wove around her so skillfully. She swallowed hard. "You sure she's not wet for you? Because that's every man's fantasy. Two women fighting each other for his cock." She broke off when he pushed a third finger into her, filling her deliciously, yet nowhere near enough. "I could make that happen, baby. Just for you."

Liam chuckled darkly. "You know better. Who would want me when they have you spread out for them?" His voice was a temptation she couldn't resist, drawing her back in despite herself. "She's crawling. Can you see her?"

"Yes," she whispered. Kenzie shivered. She'd had three-somes—and moresomes—before, but this felt different. So fucking different.

"She's stopping right between our spread legs, and she runs her hands up your thighs, moving closer until you can feel her breath on your clit. I'm pinning your hips, filling you with my cock, but keeping you still for her. She's got her lips painted…"

"Pink," Kenzie moaned. Her hips moved without her permission, seeking his hand, his cock, the mouth of the imaginary woman he'd put in the room with them.

"That first swipe of her tongue is tentative. Tasting." His voice lowered, rough and filled with the kind of desire she had coursing through her. His cock pressed against her hip, so hard.

She needed him inside her. Kenzie gripped the headboard so hard, her hands cramped.

"Liam."

"Not yet." He kissed her shoulder. "Will you come for her, Kenzie? Let her suck on that pretty little clit of yours, let her mark you up with her mouth while I'm buried deep inside?" He kissed her neck, her jawline, and spoke the next words right against her lips. "If you're very, very good, I'll let you lay her on the bed and clean up that mess you made of her pussy. Can't leave her wanting and needy, can you?" He captured her bottom lip, setting his teeth against it just hard enough to sting. "I'll fuck you from behind while you do. If you make her orgasm before you come apart on my cock, I'll give you something special as a reward."

It was too much.

She wanted what he described. Wanted it so badly she could almost taste the other woman. Kenzie released the headboard and pulled Liam on top of her. She reached between them, desperate to get rid of his hands and have his cock inside her.

Liam caught her wrist.

Kenzie blinked at him, desire a drug in her system she had no way to combat. He took his other hand, his fingers still wet with her desire, and captured her chin, guiding her face to the side. It took her several long seconds to realize what she was seeing.

The clock.

Nine fifty-five.

He won. Again.

"Oh, shit," she breathed.

Liam flipped her over onto her stomach and covered her with his body. He wedged his hand between her and the bed to finger her again. "I'll give you want you need, Kenzie. I'll always give you what you need."

Pleasure wound tighter and tighter through her, driven

on by his words and his touch and the fantasy he'd woven around her. "I need your cock," she gasped.

"You get my cock when you earn it." He kissed the back of her neck. Her fucking toes curled, and she came with a sob as she ground against his touch. So good and yet not enough. How dare he spin this fantasy around her, touch her like this, and deny them both the finish they rightly deserved?

Liam moved off her, but he didn't roll away like she expected. He pulled her to his chest and tucked her under his arm. Kenzie drifted her hand down his stomach, but he caught her wrist several inches from her destination. "No."

"But—"

"You don't get my cock, Kenzie. Not in any form."

She lifted her head and glared. "You're going to just sit there with your blue balls and suffer out of spite?"

"The end justifies the means."

Something she believed wholeheartedly, but she'd never been denied like this. Kenzie didn't like it... But she couldn't argue with how much the power games turned her on. In her years on the island, she'd given into every whim, tested out every fantasy, played every game.

Except this.

Kenzie didn't submit.

Submission required trust and that wasn't a trait she had in abundance. She let her head drop to Liam's chest and her body go limp. "I don't trust you." She couldn't tell if she was trying to convince herself or convince him.

"You don't have to trust me with everything to trust me on this—I'll never hurt you, Kenzie."

He couldn't promise that. *No one* could promise that.

She closed her eyes, exhaustion threatening to roll right over her. "Most guys wouldn't spin a scenario like that. They'd want to fuck both women."

His laugh rumbled through his chest. "Do you want me to fuck someone else while I'm in bed with you?"

She let herself picture it. What was the harm in that? Of their fantasy woman riding Liam's cock while Kenzie rode his mouth. Of knowing he did it because she wanted it. Her body clenched. "I could get down with that."

Sleep pulled at her, tugging her down into darkness. But she could have sworn she heard him murmur, "Anything for you, Kenzie. Anything."

CHAPTER 6

*L*iam woke up alone. He opened his eyes and touched the side of the bed Kenzie had spent the night curled up on. Cold. He sat up and looked around, half expecting to find that she'd taken his shit again. Nothing looked disturbed, but that didn't mean much. Last time, he hadn't even realized his wallet was missing until he went to check out of the hotel and pay for the room. *That* had been a fun conversation when Aiden arrived to pick him up. Liam shook his head at the memory.

Everyone in Boston thought he'd lost his fucking mind. He was the calm one, the steady one, the ever-present shadow to the head of the O'Malley family. Liam and Aiden might be friends, but he never forgot that the man's safety was his responsibility. It shocked everyone when he took a trip to New York and came back informing them that he'd need time off because he had to chase a ghost from his past. The only person he'd told the full truth to was Aiden, for obvious reasons, and though his friend claimed to understand, he just as clearly didn't.

How could he? His woman had all but fallen into his lap

through a strange twist of fate, and Aiden hadn't hesitated to get that locked down and put a ring on her finger as fast as humanly possible. All the O'Malley siblings were like that. Their paths might have taken them to some strange places over the years, but every single one of them managed a love match.

Last year Liam had taken a look around and…

No use thinking about it now. He had more immediate concerns than the actions that put him on this path. He was here. That was all that mattered.

He took a quick shower and pulled on another of his suits. Time to find Kenzie and remind her of their bet. She didn't seem the type to dodge the terms, not when she made such a spectacle out of the whole thing, but Liam still couldn't quite get a read on her. She constantly did the unexpected.

Like the note taped to the inside of his room door at eye level with two words scrawled on it. *The Arena.* Liam pulled it down, folded it, and tucked it into his pocket. He considered changing, but if she wanted a rematch, she'd have to wait until the seven days were up. Then he was more than happy to renegotiate—and do whatever it took to stay on the island until they saw this through to its conclusion.

He wasn't sure what that conclusion looked like.

When Liam had come to the island, it was so he could win the Wild Hunt and secure Death's favor—and use that help him track down the woman from his past. He hadn't expected said woman to be part of the Four Horsemen. It complicated things. Even if he and Kenzie somehow managed to stop circling each other long enough to carve out the possibility of a future… What would that even look like?

His life was in Boston. His *everything* was in Boston.

Hers was here.

He set it aside. There was absolutely no reason to worry

about that shit until they figured out if they could hold down a conversation. They had chemistry for days and matched up sexually, but he'd already known that coming here.

This early, Pleasure's casino floor was mostly empty except for a few die hards at the poker table. Liam skirted them and headed for the arena. He took a few wrong turns, but managed to find his way without having to pull any of the staff aside and ask for help. He hesitated in the back room, his attention snagging on the crate where he'd almost fucked Kenzie yesterday. Was it only yesterday? It felt like a small lifetime ago.

Loud music blared from the direction of the arena entrance, and Liam cautiously approached. He breathed a small sigh of relief to find the stands empty. All the lights were up, and he wasn't the least bit surprised to find that the seats appeared to recline and be well cushioned. Nothing as mundane as stadium seating for the people who frequented this place.

He belatedly recognized the song as *Pour Some Sugar on Me* and shook his head. Of course. Movement caught his attention and he zeroed in on Kenzie and she bounced on bare feet in the arena. She wore a similar outfit as she'd had on yesterday, tiny black shorts and a bright pink sports bra, and had her long blond hair back into a ponytail. The sheen of sweat on her skin said she'd been at this awhile.

She and a man circled each other in the ring, and he belatedly recognized Pestilence. He moved with an easy grace that hadn't been apparent outside the ring. It allowed him to dodge Kenzie's flurry of strikes, moving the barest amount of distance out of the way to avoid contact. It was strangely beautiful.

The beauty ceased to matter to Liam as the other man went on the attack. *He* wasn't holding back in this fight. He caught her in the shoulder, the contact pushing her off-center just enough that she never saw the sweep coming. It knocked her legs out from under her and she hit the ring hard enough to make Liam wince.

When she didn't immediately get up, he started forward.

Pestilence, naturally, got there before Liam had gone two steps. He leaned over and looked down at Kenzie. Checking in on her? Asking her if she'd had enough? Maybe talking some shit?

Impossible to say.

She shoved to her feet, her body obviously stiff enough that this wasn't the first fall she'd taken. He could practically hear the word she mouthed. *Again.*

He should stop this. Sparring was a great workout, but she was obviously punishing herself. Or maybe she had a masochistic streak. It wasn't as if Liam would know one way or another at this point. He took another step forward, but stopped short when he felt the presence of someone at his back. He turned to find Death standing there, her expression impassive.

This was the closest he'd ever been to her. On the surface, there was nothing overtly dangerous about her. She was a pretty Asian woman with long black hair and dark red lips, and she wore an expertly tailored suit that looked like it might have started off modeled after menswear, but had gotten inspired somewhere along the way. The jacket, in particular, had something funky going on with the shoulders and flared out from her small waist. A pair of red heels that matched her lips completed the look and added a good four inches to her petite stature. She had to be maybe an inch or two above five feet and one hundred pounds soaking wet.

For all that, she sent every alarm bell in his head blaring a warning he knew better than to ignore.

She eyed him. "Walk with me."

He'd been in his line of work long enough to know when

a command was framed as a request, and this was exactly that. It honestly surprised him that she'd taken this long to seek him out. Death didn't seem the type to leave anything up to chance, and Liam represented a potential snag in whatever plans they had spinning out as a result of the Wild Hunt.

She opened a door he hadn't noticed before and motioned for him to precede her. He didn't want her at his back, but he didn't appear to have a choice in the matter. Liam stepped through the door.

It led to a short hallway that turned at a ninety-degree angle. He realized where they must be—the private hallway that led to the box seats.

Sure enough, Death moved around him and led the way to a door that Liam judged to be directly centered over the arena floor. The room was smaller than other box seats he'd seen, but twice as luxurious. A full bar took up one corner and there were deep seats that overlooked the arena.

This was where the Four Horsemen watched their entertainment.

"Drink?"

"No, thanks."

She nodded as if she expected nothing less. Death motioned to the chairs. "Sit."

Liam sat. She took the one directly on his left, and her gaze went to where Kenzie and Pestilence went round again. "You seem to have a problem taking no for an answer, Liam Neale."

He sat back and forced himself to relax. "That's between me and Kenzie."

"Wrong. Anything that happens on this island is my concern—and my siblings' concern. Kenzie isn't the only one of us you have to deal with." She tapped a finger against the expensive leather of the chair. "But she's made her choice, and I'll respect it. For now."

What was he supposed to say to that?

Apparently Death didn't need a response. She finally looked at him, her dark eyes cold and uncanny. "If you harm her through intention or carelessness, I'll kill you."

"She doesn't want me dead." He didn't know why he said it, but he couldn't quite manage to keep his mouth shut.

Death smiled, the expression almost sad. "No, she doesn't. It's the only reason you're still breathing, and that leniency dissolves the second you step out of line."

Liam looked at her, really *looked* at her. "Taking the protective older sibling role a little far, aren't you?"

"Hardly." She rose smoothly. "There isn't anything I wouldn't do for my family, Liam Neale. You, of all people, should understand that line in the sand, considering where you come from. Kenzie has suffered enough for a few lifetimes. If I can keep her from hurting more in this one, I'll do it." She walked away. A few seconds later, the door to the box seats clicked shut.

Liam leaned forward and braced his elbows on his thighs, watching Kenzie take Pestilence to the ground and hop back to her feet. He should probably be pissed about Death's threat, but in the end it raised more questions that he didn't have answers to.

No one knew where the Horsemen came from. They obviously weren't related by blood, but they were a unit stronger than most families. They had created the Island of Ys, a playground to the rich and powerful, with a sterling reputation for discretion and being able to provide a person's every fantasy. People speculated on their history, but in the end all that mattered was the services they provided.

Death's word hinted at something more. That maybe the way they found each other wasn't the stuff of fairy tales—or at least not the sanitized versions.

Kenzie had suffered.

He sat back. She wouldn't tell him the truth if he asked. The woman was all smoke and mirrors, violent and beautiful and laughing and threatening. A person didn't pick up and discard traits like that unless they'd developed the skill as a coping mechanism. He knew that. Of course he knew that.

He simply hadn't considered what it meant when it came to Kenzie.

He couldn't force her to confide in him. Great sexual chemistry aside, she had no reason to trust him. Could he earn that trust in the time he'd been given?

Liam didn't know, but he'd damn well try.

* * *

KENZIE'S whole body felt like Jell-O. She lay in the middle of the ring and gasped for breath. Usually, it only took two or three rounds before she lost the uncomfortable buzzing beneath her skin and settled. Today, she and Ryu had gone a full five before he needed to get back to work. It didn't help.

It was more than losing *again* to Liam last night. They might not have had sex, but he'd made her come enough times that she should be satisfied. Orgasms were orgasms, dick involved or not.

Except that logic didn't seem to have a place here.

Or maybe it was Liam himself causing this feeling?

She opened her eyes at the sound of footsteps coming toward the ring. Kenzie rolled onto her side and found Liam staring at her, an unreadable expression on his handsome face. "Late sleeper."

"I was waylaid." He shrugged. "I'm here now."

Waylaid by Amarante, no doubt. Even if Ryu hadn't been occupied sparring with Kenzie for the last hour or so, he preferred not to make his threats face to face. In fact, he rarely made them at all. If someone crossed the line, he simply acted and that was that. No one saw him coming. Amarante usually gave some kind of warning if the person wasn't an active enemy. A courtesy before she took them out at the knees, which was very old world of her.

It sure as hell wasn't Luca, not with him *still* in Thalania. He was supposed to be back a week ago and yet somehow he hadn't managed it yet. Not that she held his happiness and apparent honeymoon phase with the princess against him.

Much.

"Come down. Let's find some breakfast."

She'd rather get right down to fucking, but the terms of the last bet lingered. *No cock for me.* She really needed to work on her impulse control. Kenzie sighed and rolled off the edge of the ring. Liam's surprised curse made her laugh as she caught the edge and leveraged herself to her feet. He'd taken three large steps toward her, as if he thought to catch her before she hit the ground.

What a novel thought.

No. No novel thoughts when it comes to this man. He's not exactly an enemy, but he's sure as hell not an ally, either.

She ignored the hand he offered and marched toward the exit. "I need a shower."

"Kenzie." The snap in his voice stopped her cold.

She spun around. "Don't do that. I'm not a dog you can call to heel just because you don't like what I have to say."

Liam, damn him, didn't give her any reaction. "Move your stuff to my room for the duration of the week."

Her jaw dropped. "You can't—"

"You'll find that I just did. You said you were mine for the week. Or did you only mean when it was convenient for you?"

How dare he question her on this? She wasn't the one being irrational. *He* kept pushing her, kept demanding more, and it hadn't even been twenty-four hours. Kenzie glared. "Fine."

"Now."

She'd make him pay for this, for the feeling akin to humiliation surging through her. She liked her space, liked having a place to retreat to that was hers and hers alone. Sleeping next to Liam...

That was the problem. She *slept* last night. No dreams. No nightmares. None of the restlessness that plagued her every hour of every day and night. She'd closed her eyes, his arm a heavy weight around her hips, his strong body at her back, and Kenzie fell into a sleep like the dead.

It scared the shit out of her.

The one conclusion she'd come to while sparring with Ryu was that she couldn't allow it to happen again...and that's exactly what Liam planned for her.

Damn him.

Kenzie felt him at her back as she walked out of the arena and into the halls. She spun around again and pointed a finger in his face. "Space, Liam. I'll dance to your tune, but you will give me some goddamn space."

He didn't blink. "You have an hour. I'll order room service."

Not even the potential promise of more orgasms could keep her temper in check. Kenzie never reacted all that well to being trapped, and the only reason she'd stomached losing the sparring bet was because she *wanted* to lose. It gave her the excuse she needed in order to take what she wanted without the appearance of giving in.

She hadn't expected Liam to cut off her retreat.

She really, really should have.

CHAPTER 7

*K*enzie took her time out of spite. She showered and dicked around for an hour before methodically packing. Liam wanted her in his room? Then he'd damn well *get* her in his room. She wondered if he'd ever lived with a woman before, if he was prepared for the sheer amount of shit Kenzie was about to implode all over his neat little world. In the end, it didn't matter. She'd obey his order, but she'd make him choke on it in the process.

Actually...

Kenzie pulled open her nightstand drawer and grabbed two vibrators to toss onto the top of her clothes. *Take that, you bastard.* She zipped her suitcase and yanked it off the bed with a thunk.

Too much to hope that the hub would be empty for her reverse walk of shame. Ryu lounged in his chair in front of his computer, typing away at a speed that made her dizzy. He glanced up and his fingers froze over the keyboard. "Going somewhere?"

"I made a very stupid decision and now I'm suffering for it."

Ryu slowly spun his chair to face her. Most people looked rumpled after a few hours in front of a screen. Not her brother. He was just as perfectly pressed as when he'd sat down, who knew how long ago. "Amarante talked to him today while we sparred."

Of all the— "She told me I had a week."

He didn't look away. "He's under your skin."

"He's not under my skin. It's been a day, Ryu. A single day. Liam isn't under anything but *me*."

Ryu shook his head. "This one's different." He sat back and tugged on his cuffs, one of the only tells he had. Sure enough, he dove right off the deep end. "He came here for you."

"What?" *Damn it, Kenzie, that was too shocked.*

He narrowed his eyes. "He came here for you," he repeated. "Which got me thinking."

"Not that."

"When the hell could you have met this mob guy? He stayed local for most of his life, and you only leave the island every so often. So I checked."

"Ryu."

He ignored her. "You were in Boston a couple years after we bought the island. Wouldn't have stuck out to me now, except I distinctly remember you cancelling your flight and rebooking it for the next day out." He met her gaze. "Is he why?"

She could lie. It would be smarter to laugh the whole thing off and pretend her brother was crazy and delusional and definitely out of line. Throw a hissy fit loud enough that even Ryu would back off his quest for the truth. There was nothing he liked better than information, especially when he viewed that information as vital in keeping them safe. He was just as bad as Amarante in his way, though he preferred a subtler approach.

Big brothers were a pain in the ass.

She propped her hands on her hips and glared. "Yes, okay, he was why. We met at bar and shared a drink and I thought he was sexy, so I banged his brains out that night and then stole his wallet the next morning." She hadn't gone *too* crazy with the theft. It wasn't like she drained all his accounts. She just charged up his credit cards.

Ryu blinked. "That's it?"

"Yes!" She threw up her hands. "That's what I've been saying. It was one night like eight years ago. I have no idea why he tracked me down."

"He didn't." He tapped his toe absently, a sure sign she was about to lose him to his computer. "He came here to ask Amarante to find you. He had no idea you were *you*."

She didn't know if that made it better or worse. In the end, it didn't matter. They had their fun then, and they'd have their fun now. He would leave and she would track down the monster from her past and put a knife in his throat. There was no other way forward, not that she could live with. "Declan still on track to arrive next week?"

"Yes." Ryu grinned so suddenly, it rocked her back on her heels. "Now that I know these three, I'm keeping close track of them. He's not doing anything out of the ordinary. There's barely any chatter about the Bookkeeper going missing."

"Good." That bitch might not have gotten her hands literally dirty, but her accounting was drenched in the blood of innocents. She deserved everything Amarante had done to her and more. "Keep me updated?"

"I will."

There was nothing left to stall with. She sighed, grabbed her suitcase, and walked out of the hub. Kenzie didn't want to draw attention to herself and her current sleeping arrangements, so she kept to the warren of passageways. It meant the trip to Liam's room took a little longer, but she was still pissed about the deadline, so she relished making him wait.

Or at least she did until she walked through his suite's door and found him sitting there, waiting for her with a strange expression on his face. She missed a step and then cursed herself for even that much reaction. In response, she fell back on her best defense.

When in doubt, go over the top.

Kenzie sent her suitcase rolling in ahead of her and spread her arms. "Honey, I'm home. Did you miss me?"

"Kenzie."

She ignored him and waltzed across the room, putting a little swing into her step. "Because I missed you."

There it was, the heat flaring in his dark eyes. He banked it almost immediately, but it was too late. He thought he could control this interaction—every interaction. Fuck that. He already knew her buttons too well, and she desperately needed some leverage, something to push him back a little, to keep him from overwhelming her.

She smiled sweetly, enjoying the way his brows slammed down in response. "I missed you, baby." Kenzie unzipped the front of her dress. She'd had a burst on inspiration after her shower and dressed to fit. The dress was black and hugged her body, but the real show was beneath it. She peeled it off as she walked slowly toward him.

His breath hitched.

His breath fucking *hitched*.

Sheer stubbornness kept her on her feet, stepping out of the dress and moving to straddle his thighs. She wore garter belt and thigh-highs and a balconette lace bra, all in black. And nothing else.

Liam didn't touch her, though he gripped the arms of the

chair hard enough she thought he might actually rip them off. "You're missing part of your wardrobe."

"Am I?" She cupped her breasts and slid her hands down to stroke her thumbs over the lace garter belt. As he watched, she dipped lower to touch her pussy. "Oh, gracious, you're right. Silly me."

"Kenzie."

She loved that growl that worked its way into his voice, a sure sign of him losing control. Kenzie gave herself a teasing stroke and braced her hands on the back of the chair, bending down so her breasts were nearly in his face. "I have something to confess."

"I'm not a priest."

"Now that would be a goddamn tragedy." She gave a little shimmy that had him doing that delicious breath hitch again. "If you were, I might make it my goal in life to corrupt you, tempt you until you fucked me right there in that holy sanctuary everyone's always going on about."

"Heathen," he murmured. He still hadn't touched her.

That wouldn't do.

Kenzie pushed off the chair and walked away, and yeah, she definitely put some swing in her walk. There was a tall mirror on the wall next to the door and she watched him watch her ass with every step. "So, about my confession." She stopped in front of the mirror and pretended to check her bright red lipstick. "I never wear panties."

"You wear a lot of short dresses for that kind of habit."

"Mmm." She smoothed a hand over her hips. "That's the attraction, Liam. Do you know how hot I get knowing that when I'm in need, there's one less barrier between me and getting what I want?" Irritation flared that he didn't react, so she escalated. "I can flirt with someone on the casino floor and, when I'm so hot I can't stand it any longer, I can take their hand and slide it under my dress. Anywhere. Anytime."

"You wicked little slut." He didn't say it like it was a bad thing. He practically growled the words as if relishing them. "Get over here."

Her skin flared hot and her body clenched. Now was the time to take control... Except Kenzie turned and walked back to him, drawn by the arrogant command. He didn't wait for her to choose. He grabbed her hand and pulled hard, sending her sprawling into him. Liam moved her before she could recover. Her back to his chest. Her legs draped over either side of his thighs. One of his hands at her throat. The other fisting the front of her garter belt. "You get off on the possibly of anyone touching you."

"Anyone I want."

"Anyone you want," he echoed. He met her gaze in the mirror. "You want me to touch you."

It wasn't even in the realm of a question, but she still nodded. "I want you to do more than touch me."

Liam nipped her neck and dipped his hand down, spreading his fingers to frame her pussy. "You want me to finger you and fuck you and lick you until your eyes roll back in your head and the only name you know is mine."

She couldn't quite catch her breath. He was so close to where she needed him, and his hard cock against her ass promised enough pleasure to beat back her earlier frustration. "I don't know if I'd put it quite like that, but—"

"No."

Kenzie blinked, sure she'd misheard him. "What?"

"No." Liam lifted her enough so he could slide out from beneath her and then dropped her onto the chair. "You are not in charge, Kenzie. Best make your peace with that."

She was going to *kill* him.

* * *

LIAM NEEDED A FUCKING DRINK. He couldn't afford to show that much faltering in front of Kenzie, though, which only served to spike his frustration higher. She thought she could manipulate him the same way she manipulated her other partners. That he'd be distracted with a hand up her skirt and forget his other goals.

It almost worked.

He stalked to the phone without looking at her. "Breakfast order?"

"I'm not hungry," she snarled.

She was pissed, but he didn't give a fuck because he was pissed, too. He snatched up the phone and ordered them a full breakfast spread, but put it on a delay. He had something to take care of before they could eat.

All Liam wanted was to sit down with this woman and have a conversation like two normal people. He should have known better. They weren't two normal people, and this wasn't anything like a normal situation. She wanted to play things this way? Fine.

Three steps, one long breath, and he clamped down on what little control he had left. He scooped up her discarded dress and grabbed the suitcase handle. Kenzie jumped up, but it was too late by then. He shoved them both into the closet and locked the door before she reached him. Liam had thought it strange that the closets functioned as safes when he first checked in, but reasoned it had to do with how much jewelry he saw on the women on the island. Now he thanked it for the resource it was.

Kenzie grabbed for the key, but he shoved it into his pocket. "You can have them back when you realize you're playing *my* game."

"You are such a bastard."

"Only when it comes to you."

She glared. "Is that supposed to be a compliment?"

"It's a statement of truth." He resisted the urge to drag his fingers through his hair. At this point, he was liable to rip it out. Words ripped from his mouth before he had a chance to think better of them. "In the living room. Hands on the coffee table."

Kenzie froze. "Excuse me?"

"You heard me."

She hesitated, as if she half expected him to take it back. Hell, *he* half expected to take it back. Liam didn't.

Finally, she walked slowly into the living room, studied the coffee table for a moment and pressed her hands flat to its surface. In her heels, it left her bent nearly in half. "Spread your legs." The command felt dragged from him.

She obeyed. "I really don't like you right now."

"Liar." He walked over and dragged a finger across her pussy. "You're so wet for me, you're practically dripping. I think you love this shit." He made himself stop touching her, made himself take a full step back. "I think you've had control so long, you're fucking exhausted and it feels good to submit, if only in this."

"You seem to think a lot," she muttered.

"Tell me I'm wrong."

"You're wrong."

He shook his head and sank back into the chair he'd originally occupied. "The only thing keeping you here is you. I haven't tied you up. I'm not threatening you. You hate this shit? Door's right there."

The muscles in her legs flexed as if she might do exactly that, but she huffed out a breath and stayed in position. "You have my clothes."

"Whatever you have to tell yourself." They both knew that wouldn't stop her. "Spread wider, Kenzie. Show me everything."

She did. The wider position allowed him a better view of

her face—and allowed her to see him. Liam held her gaze as he unzipped his pants and pulled out his cock. The shock in those hazel eyes was almost worth the fact he was about to jack himself instead of sinking into her wet heat. He gave himself a rough stroke and then another, letting himself sink into the perfection of the picture she presented. She shivered, which made it even better.

"Liam." She licked her lips. "Liam, I need you."

"No." He was so wound up, pleasure already sparked through him, a building pressure he didn't bother to hold back. He came hard, cursing himself and cursing her in the process. It couldn't be fucking *simple* with them. He was a goddamn fool for thinking it could.

He stood and made his way into the bedroom. As tempting as it was to rush through changing, he forced himself to take his time, to punish both of them for getting to this point.

Kenzie remained exactly where he'd left her.

Perfection. She was fucking perfection.

He stalked to stand behind her. "Tell me something." Liam palmed her ass, coasting his hands down over her until his thumbs brushed her pussy. He gave her a squeeze, which made her moan. "Is sex pleasure or punishment?"

"I don't understand the question."

Yes, she damn well did. He went to his knees behind her and parted her with his thumbs. "All those people you fuck with such abandon. Is it because you love sex that much? Or are you running from something and that's the way you deal with it?"

She arched her back, tilting her hips down to offer herself to him. He didn't think she even realized she'd made the move, but he rewarded it with a long lick. Kenzie shivered. "More."

"Answer the question."

"Fuck you!" She yipped when he swatted her ass, just hard enough to make it sting. Liam immediately gave her pussy another slow drag of his tongue, and Kenzie shook as if she couldn't decide whether to pull away or push back against him. Her breath shuddered out. "It's both, you dickhead. I love it. I love being able to crook my finger at someone, man or woman, and have them panting after me."

He pulled back long enough to demand, "The rest?"

She cursed, but she answered on a moan. "It helps me breathe, okay? It keeps me from going out of my skin, and when I can't fuck, I fight."

That was enough for now. Liam gave himself over to the taste of her, to her rising moans every time he speared his tongue into her pussy. She was just as tightly wound as he was, because several short minutes later she came, her body going taunt and her arms giving out. He pulled her back before she face-planted on the table, ending up on the floor with her in his arms. Kenzie tried to pull away, but he wasn't about to allow a retreat. Not yet.

Liam gathered her to his chest and tucked her head under his chin. Several seconds later, when it became clear he had no intention of continuing the interrogation, she relaxed against him. He held her until he could feel her heartbeat slow and their breathing returned to normal.

Someone knocked on the door. "A minute," Liam called.

He rose awkwardly to his feet, ignoring Kenzie's comment that she could walk, and carried her into the bedroom. It was quick work to find one of the two robes hanging on the bathroom door and tuck her into it.

She sighed. "This really isn't necessary."

"I really don't give a fuck." Satisfied she was covered, he went to open the door and allow room service in. They'd made progress just now, which meant Kenzie would be trying to retreat. He had to figure out a way to stop them from taking one step forward and two steps back. Hell, as he tipped the room service guy and closed the door, he half expected to find she'd disappeared somehow.

But Kenzie was still there, looking strangely small and vulnerable in the fluffy white robe. He wanted to go to her, to hold her again, but Liam knew enough by now to know that she wouldn't accept any kind of comfort but the type associated with sex.

He pointed at the breakfast spread. "Pancakes?"

CHAPTER 8

*K*enzie felt like she'd been dragged behind a car. Not in a physical sense. Nothing he'd done had actually hurt her. He'd simply pulled information from her that she'd had no intention of sharing.

Responses from her that she'd never intended to share.

She poked at her breakfast, her gaze straying back to the coffee table where she'd planted her hands and submitted. A first for her. Kenzie might know her way around a sex dungeon—she was partial owner of Pain, after all—but she'd never chosen to be on this side of things. It was too closely linked to the feeling of being trapped, of being out of control. Rationally, she knew the submissive ultimately held the upper hand in any power games, but that didn't change how raw she felt right now.

As if he'd broken her wide open.

She wanted, needed, to get back on stable ground. Since she couldn't best him in fucking, it would have to be fighting. Kenzie set down her fork. "However this plays out in your head, reality won't work like that. We don't have a future."

"So you've said. Several times." Liam didn't sound the

least bit concerned about it. He drank his coffee and watched her with an unreadable expression on his face. "Tell me about how you found the others."

She started to shut him down, but forced herself to stop. He'd systematically overridden every defense mechanism she had, constantly turning the tables in his favor. She couldn't evade indefinitely. There were still five days left, and if he could unravel her this thoroughly in forty-eight hours, then she didn't like her chances to remain unscathed for the rest of the duration.

Maybe knowing her truth would be enough to get him to back off, to see that this could be a really sexy fling, but that ultimately it couldn't go anywhere. "When I was a kid, I was sold to a group of traffickers that, in turn, sold me to a camp up in Canada. A very particular place for people with specific interests."

"Kenzie," he whispered. Just that. Nothing more.

She ignored it, striving for the nonchalance she *should* feel after all this time. "I was a pretty kid, even then, and so I fit a particular type they were looking for." Even twenty years later, she could still taste the panic on her tongue when they shoved her into that room, dressed like a little doll. "I didn't play by the rules. I couldn't stop fighting them, couldn't lie there and take it the way some of the kids managed." She gave a mirthless smile. "I was never that good at checking out mentally."

Liam didn't speak, didn't seem to breathe. Just as well. If he tried to touch her now, she couldn't be held accountable. She idly picked up the butter knife and examined it. "That's what drew Death and Pestilence to me. They'd been there longer than I had, suffered differently, but like calls to like. I wouldn't lie down and die, not emotionally and sure as fuck not physically. They taught me how to survive, how to keep as much of myself locked away as I could. And when we escaped that place, we kept each other alive. I owe them *everything*."

He was silent for a beat, two. "And the ones responsible?"

Kenzie finally looked at him. "Why? Are you going to set your mob connections on them? Wipe them from the face of the earth?"

"You don't fuck with kids, Kenzie. Hell, you don't fuck with innocents." He stared at her, dark eyes hard and unknowable. If she saw that face on the other side of a gun, she'd know she'd breathed her last. It sent a thrill through her that wasn't entirely unpleasant.

Kenzie had always had a weakness for strength.

She set the knife down carefully. "This story doesn't have that kind of happy ending, Liam. They wore masks, always and without exception. Other than a few defining traits, I couldn't tell you enough to find even one of the responsible parties." At least, she wouldn't have been able to until they'd taken the Bookkeeper last week. Now, the whole game board had changed. There was a chance for justice. True justice.

There was a chance to keep more children from going through what she and the others had gone through.

"I see." His tone said the conversation wasn't closed, and she had no doubt that he'd be making a call back to Boston to set one of their tech geeks on tracking down any information about this place that he could find.

She'd have told him it was a lost cause, but her chest felt strange at the thought of Liam being that determined to take down someone that hurt her—hurt innocents. "There's nothing you can do."

He shrugged. "Time will tell."

Damn it, this was supposed to damage his intentions to get close to her, not cement them. She flopped back on the couch and sighed. "You make it really difficult to hate you, you know that?"

"You don't need to hate me, Kenzie. I'm not going to hurt you." *Not like the others* went unsaid.

She could have kept going, could have told him about how they got set up with this place, how they slowly built a life for themselves here, how she'd fought tooth and nail back from the edge of despair in those early years on the island. Falling into the emotional pit was akin to letting the bastards win.

She found ways to cope because she had no other choice. She threw herself into life with a fury that startled people. She lived every moment like it might be her last. She fought and fucked and fought some more. She learned to be an entertainer, learned how to hold an audience on the edge of their seats. It was *her* skillset that brought the Island of Ys to the next level. First while playing the White Stag in the Wild Hunt, and then again with the various events she organized and pulled off to draw in more people—and their money.

Were her coping skills the healthiest? Hell no. A therapist would have a field day with her. But they worked and they kept her going. It was enough. It had to be enough.

She sat up. "Honey, you couldn't hurt me if you tried."

Liar.

Liam studied her for a long moment, and finally shook his head. "Noted." He pushed to his feet. "What else is there to do on this island?"

She blinked. The conversation was over? Just like that? He didn't want to delve deep into her psyche and pull her apart for his curiosity? "Swimming?"

"Swimming works." He jerked his thumb over his shoulder at the closet where he'd locked up her clothes. "You have a suit in there?"

"Yes, of course." Even though she worked long hours between the casinos, she made an effort to hit the water at least once every few days. Swimming in the ocean didn't bring about the same feeling as running through the big island, narrowly avoiding the competitors hunting her, but it scratched the itch. The ocean wasn't tamed, could never be tamed, and she loved it.

"Let's go."

She didn't immediately move when he pushed to his feet. "I don't understand you."

"Only one way to change that." He held out his hand. "Let's go," Liam repeated.

Kenzie didn't give herself a chance to think. She simply took his hand and allowed him to pull her to her feet.

* * *

LIAM SPENT the whole ride to Kenzie's preferred beach chewing on the new information rattling around in his head. He'd suspected that the Horsemen were brought together by ill deeds. People didn't bond like that, didn't arise from nowhere, didn't become forces of nature because they had a happy and content home life. He still hadn't expected...

He hadn't expected a lot of things when it came to Kenzie.

She related it all so personally, as if the trauma was something delivered to someone on a screen. None of the iced-out distance he'd seen in others. None of the messy emotional stuff. Just... It happened, and now it's over.

He wanted to kill whoever had hurt her. Because it was her, yes, but also because it took a special kind of monster to prey on a child. Liam wasn't a good man, and he'd done things that paved the way to hell, rather than heaven, but there were still lines that shouldn't be crossed.

"Stop that."

He glanced at Kenzie. She handled their little golf cart with ease, sending them flying alone the dirt trail through the trees. She seemed just as relaxed as ever, her masks firmly back in place. "Stop what?"

"Stop brooding. I was proving a point before, and now it's done. You wanted to get out of the casino, and here we are. Smile. It won't break your face. Probably."

Tempted to fall into her teasing, to let her push away the darkness of his thoughts, Liam sighed. He wouldn't win her by acting like this, but the situation felt like quicksand. The more he tried to find a way forward, the faster he sank. "Where are we headed?"

She gave him a look like the change of subject didn't fool her. "A private beach. The tourists have the boardwalk between Pleasure and Pain, and they have the west side of the island with the villas there. This is just ours." Kenzie glanced at the trail and maneuvered them around a giant pothole. "Well, I guess it's mine. My siblings aren't really outside kids, if you know what I mean."

"I guess I do. I get Death and Pestilence." They were both icy enough to be statues breathed to life, and Liam had a hard time imagining them doing any leisure activities. "But Famine seems like more a rough and tumble guy."

"He is," she answered easily. "And he comes out here with me sometimes, but the jungle gets to be a bit much for him." A shadow passed over her expression. "He shouldn't have entered the Wild Hunt. It had to have his skeletons rattling around in his closet."

Another token of the past, no doubt.

Liam started to ask another question, but the words died as they shot from the trees and took a hard right. They'd reached the beach. His breath whooshed out. "It's perfect."

"I know."

White sand stretched down into impossibly blue water. Kenzie guided the cart to a stop next to a small, sturdy shack. She hopped down and went to unlock it, reappearing seconds later with a couple chairs and shoving an umbrella into his hands. "You look like you burn."

"Thanks?"

She grinned and headed down the beach to set up the chairs, leaving Liam to follow her.

He didn't trust this new Kenzie, didn't trust that this perky attitude was anything less than a retreat. He could keep pushing, or he could give her a moment to find her feet, to see what the day would bring. Liam checked the sky. Clear and blue and just as perfect as their surroundings.

He headed to her and they set up the umbrella. Kenzie unwrapped her swimsuit coverup thing and dropped it onto the chair, giving Liam the first good look at her.

Fuck.

She'd lied. She didn't have a suit. She was fucking naked.

Kenzie saw him looking and laughed. "Suits are for decency, and I think we've both proven we have none." She grinned. "Besides, tan lines are the worst." She turned and strode down the beach and straight into the water, disappearing beneath the surface.

She was going to kill him.

Every time he thought he knew her next step, she did something to totally knock him on his ass. Liam took a deep breath and looked around. He wasn't a prude, exactly, but he'd never bothered to check skinny dipping off his bucket list.

Kenzie surfaced, her laugh reaching him across the distance. That decided him more than anything. Liam shucked off his suit and followed her into the water.

She grinned, something softening in her expression for the first time since he'd arrived on the island. "Told you so."

"That tan lines are the worst?"

"No." She splashed him. "That we have no decency."

He couldn't exactly argue that, so he didn't bother. Liam

contented himself with floating in the salt water and letting it ease something he hadn't even been aware was tense. "I've never swam in the ocean."

She sputtered. "*Never?* You live in Boston. You're *on* the ocean."

"It's different there." He considered. "At least superficially. We were on the verge of war for a long time."

"Yeah, yeah, I know." She waved that away. "But you were a child at some point, I'm assuming. Your parents never took you down to Jersey or wherever people in Boston go to vacation?"

Liam shook his head slowly. "My parents were employed by the O'Malleys. They were paid more than fairly enough, but it doesn't leave a lot of room for vacation." The only thing that counted, maybe, was accompanying Aiden to the Connecticut house from time to time during the summers. But even as a kid, Liam knew his place. He wasn't an O'Malley, didn't hold the same position of power. He was support, plain and simple, someone to have Aiden's back, to ensure that his plans played out accordingly. A truth that only solidified as they became adults and Aiden stepped up to head the family.

"What a pair we make." She laughed again, though it felt more strained this time. "Questionable childhoods and a total mess as adults."

He started to argue but… She wasn't wrong. He'd been trained from childhood to be Aiden's right hand. It wasn't normal by any stretch of the imagination. He liked to think his parents hadn't tried to get pregnant on purpose to ensure they had an extra in with the family, but he couldn't put it past them.

"You said 'were' about your parents. Are they still around?" It was as if she plucked the thought right from his head.

"No. My mom died when I was a teenager. My dad a few years after that. Cancer and car crash, respectively."

"Oh." He thought it might end there, but she kept going. "What was it like? Having parents?"

Liam didn't glance at her, didn't give her a chance to take the tentative question back. "Like you said, we had questionable childhoods. They weren't bad people. They never knocked me around or any of that shit. They just had their priorities set on other things. Power. Influence. Whatever. They never got what they wanted." He'd seen their ambition reflected in so much of what they taught him. It was sheer dumb luck that he and Aiden ended up as friends, and he'd hated their attempts to use that relationship to their advantage.

"I never want kids." She smoothed back her wet hair. "I might have worked through a lot of my shit, but there's no way I wouldn't screw up a tiny person relying only on me. I think some people should just not procreate."

He opened his mouth to tell her she might change her mind, and shut it. "I don't know if I want kids, either." He stopped moving so suddenly, he went under. Liam pushed back to the surface and swiped a hand over his face. "I don't think I've ever admitted that before."

Kenzie gave him a look. "What's the big deal?"

"The family I work for, the O'Malleys, tends toward breeding like it's their responsibility to repopulate the world." He laughed a little. "I have nearly a dozen honorary nieces and nephews at this point. I like kids. I just don't know if that's my path."

"Look at you, breaking the mold and all that jazz." She twisted to look back at the beach and a strange expression came over her face. "Well, shit."

He followed her gaze and went still. A man stood on the beach next to their cart, his arms crossed over his chest. Even from the distance, Liam recognized him. Dark hair, dark eyes, the kind of bearing that would make Liam think twice about going a round or two.

Apparently Famine was back on the island.

* * *

KENZIE SIGHED and glanced back at the open ocean behind her. Swimming until she couldn't swim any longer and sinking into a watery grave was preferable to the lecture she had coming. Amarante was content to let her do this. Ryu argued and asked questions she didn't want to answer, but he trusted her to find her own way.

Luca was going to kick her ass.

"Kenzie?"

She didn't look at Liam. "Come on. Time to pay the piper." She moved quickly, ignoring Liam's strangled curse, and walked out of the water to the chairs. Luca cut her a look that wasn't the least bit sexual in nature. No, he was checking her body for signs of injury. In that single glance, she knew he'd catalogued her various bruises. She snatched up her cover-up and wrapped it around her body. "What's with the storm cloud you have hovering around your head? I thought your princess would have fucked that bad mood right out of you."

"She did." Luca watched Liam approach, his dark eyes narrowed. "Then I get back here and find out you're fucking around with this idiot—and Te is letting you."

She propped her hands on her hips and glared. "You know she's not our mother, right? We're all on the same playing field."

He snorted. "Sure, Kenzie. Keep telling yourself that."

The worst part? He was right. Amarante might be their sister, but she ruled them all in her way. They didn't step out of line without her permission, and they all cleaved to her plan to bring down their enemy. Luca had his own reasons for doing that. Ryu had a lifetime of being the younger sibling and following Amarante's orders.

Kenzie did it because she owed Amarante everything. She wouldn't have survived six months in that place on her own, let alone the five years she ended up being there. Amarante had earned her loyalty, and once given, that wasn't something Kenzie took back.

Liam pulled on his pants. Only once he was covered did he start in on Luca. "This is none of your business."

"Wrong. This is my little sister and my island. That makes it my business."

"Oh, for fuck's sake." Kenzie rolled her eyes. "Get your dicks out and swing them around on your own time. You." She pointed at Luca. "You might be my brother, but you know better than to pull this overprotective bullshit. Knock it off. And you." She turned to Liam. "He *is* my brother and that means you can't pull any of that heavy-handed bullshit."

Both men looked like they wanted to challenge her words, but she refused to give them a chance. She snapped her fingers. "Liam, get in the cart."

From the way the muscle jumped in his jaw, she'd pay for this later. So be it. Kenzie waited for him to follow her order before she tuned back to Luca. "I have five days."

"Kenzie—"

"Has something changed that requires a shorter timeline?"

He finally shook his head. "Not that I'm aware of."

"Good. Then back the fuck off. I don't need you to protect me."

Luca gave a small smile. "You're the most capable of all of us."

That was a flat out lie, but she still liked hearing it. Kenzie had no illusions about her skillset. She couldn't lie to herself and still pull off the various events she participated in on the island. She had to be able to identify her strengths and weaknesses and be honest about it. That meant she knew beyond a shadow of a doubt that she wasn't the most capable of the Horsemen. She was a valuable asset to their foursome, but without Ryu's technical magic, they wouldn't have had the money to create this place. Without Luca, they couldn't keep it safe. Without Amarante, *none* of this would have happened to begin with.

But Luca was trying to cheer her up, and so she couldn't totally shoot him down. "Did Cami come back with you?"

"Yeah." He studied her for several moments. "You okay with this?"

"Okay with you falling for an honest to god princess and chasing her across half the world to tell her that you loved her and beg her to come back here and be your lady?" Kenzie laughed, though the sound wasn't nearly as vibrant as usual. "Of course, Luca. I'm happy for you. Legit happy."

The look he gave her said he saw through her, but he finally nodded. "Sometimes change isn't bad."

Why is it okay for you to fall for someone, but not for me?

Kenzie shut that thought down almost as soon as it rose. What happened with Luca and Cami was different. The woman had been looking for something, and she'd found it in Kenzie's brother. It wasn't anything like Liam tracking down Kenzie. *Liam* had a life, had loyalties of his own.

They had no future. She knew that. He'd know that, too, if he'd stop being so stubborn.

"I have to go."

"Be careful with him."

She laughed. "You know better." Kenzie smacked him on the shoulder. "Be a darling and put these chairs away, would you?" She ignored his muttered curse and strode to the cart where Liam sat.

He was still watching Luca. "Everything okay?"

"Why wouldn't it be okay? I deflected a pissing match and got a lecture from my overprotective big brother." She floored it, sending them flying back down the dirt trail. If Luca was back, it meant things were moving forward as planned.

It meant her time with Liam would come to a close all too soon.

She had to make every moment count.

"Liam?"

"Yes?"

Kenzie kept her attention on the trail, her hands gripping the steering wheel hard enough that her knuckles went white. "Is there a reason you're denying us what we both want? You're right—I like the power games and the betting and all that shit. But we don't have forever. We only have right now. And right now I need you."

I need you.

Words she hadn't meant to say.

Words she meant.

"Pull over."

Kenzie sped up and veered around a little offshoot trail. It went up toward the dock they used to bring the White Stag to the large island for the Wild Hunt. The rest of the year, it wasn't used much at all, and it sure as hell wouldn't be today. She still drove several agonizing minutes up it, ensuring that Luca wouldn't happen across them when he drove back to Pleasure.

She'd barely stopped the cart when Liam hauled her up to straddle him. He kissed her as if he hadn't had his mouth all over her body a few short hours ago. Like he'd never get enough. She kissed him back just as fiercely, trying to convey her need without speaking a word.

He understood.

Of course he understood.

Liam pushed her wrap aside enough to bare her from the waist down. He slid a finger into her and growled when he found her ready. She broke the kiss long enough to say, "Please Liam. Just…please."

He clasped the back of her neck and brought her mouth to his again, but he answered her plea by using his other to free his cock. She half expected hesitation, something like the teasing torture he'd delivered to her time and time again. Liam gave her none of it. He notched his cock at her entrance and she slammed down on him.

The sheer size of him left her gasping. The only other time they had sex on the island, she'd been an orgasm in before he ever got inside her. Kenzie shivered, trying to adjust to his size. She loved this. She loved this so fucking much. Riding the edge between pain and pleasure, his rough hands on her body, his mouth against hers, demanding more.

Yes, yes, yes, yes.

She rolled her hips, taking him deeper. The hint of pain disappeared, leaving only the need to move, to fuck him out here where anyone could see. No one would, but that didn't matter. She shrugged the straps of her wrap off her shoulders, letting it fall to bare her breasts.

Liam kissed along her jaw and down her neck, but he sat back before he reached her breasts. His dark eyes went searing hot. "Ride me, Kenzie. Give me a show and take what you need."

She looked down her body, enjoying the sight as much as he obviously did. Her wrap was a tangle across her stomach and her exposed breasts bounced each time she slammed down on him. But the view of his cock sliding into her? That had her pleasure rising to an almost unbearable level. "You're so big, baby."

"Made just for you, Kenzie. Big and thick to make your pussy feel so fucking good." He stopped touching her and draped his arms over the back of the cart's seat. "Use me. That's what you need, isn't it? Ride my cock, finger that sensitive little clit until you come all over me."

She did exactly as he commanded, feeling more than a little wicked to be fucking him like this without him touching her, to *use* him even as he enjoyed the hell out of it. Kenzie reached behind her to brace a hand on the front of the cart and slid her other hand down to finger her clit. She was so close, seemed to constantly be dancing on the edge with Liam. Even as part of her wanted to make this last, to draw it out, she couldn't have stopped even if she wanted to. Her orgasm hit her, bowing her back and drawing a strangled cry from her lips.

Only then did Liam touch her. He grabbed her hips and used her body to fuck his cock, following her over the edge a few moments later. He pulled Kenzie down against his chest and wrapped his arms around her.

She had the dazed thought that she should put a stop to this cuddling nonsense, but it felt good to be wrapped up in him.

Safe.

Like maybe she belonged there.

It wasn't the truth, couldn't be the truth, but she still allowed herself to close her eyes and believe the lie. If only for a little while.

CHAPTER 9

*L*iam's need for Kenzie was a fire in his blood. They barely got back to his room before he had her against the door, his cock buried deep inside her. Having her clench around him, her body moving against his in a rhythm as natural as breathing, her cries in his ear as she came... It only stoked his need higher.

He couldn't stop. He didn't want to. Control had taken a backseat days ago, and Liam felt more animal than man as he finished and then hauled Kenzie to the bed to begin again. Every time she came, it felt like another tether attaching them. It wasn't the truth, but he needed that tether all the same.

Kenzie, for her part, seemed just as desperate for him.

They finally slipped into an exhausted sleep sometime later, Liam's body giving out before his will did. Having her tucked against his larger body felt right, too. It all felt fucking right.

She woke him in the night with her mouth around his cock.

Liam hissed out a breath and laced his fingers through

her hair, content to let her take control this time. To take care of him in her own way.

She moved over him slowly as if she loved every second of it, taking him deep and then shallow, licking and sucking and then running the head of his cock over her lips. "Fuck," he breathed.

"It's not morning." She did it again. "Go back to sleep."

"Mmm." He gave her hair a little tug. "I'll do that."

"Good." She took him deep again and then deeper yet, sucking him down until her lips met his base. Liam cursed again. He couldn't help it.

She lifted her head. "You're not going back to sleep, are you?" The teasing in her tone made him smile despite how fucking hard his cock was.

"Somehow, it's not happening." He tugged her hair again. "Come here."

"Impatient."

"Only when it comes to you."

She smacked his hands away. "Stop that. I want to suck your dick, and I want to drink you down when you come."

He'd thought it impossible for his cock to get harder. He'd been wrong. "Kenzie."

"I know that tone, baby, but you can't have my pussy right now." She slid back down to make a fist around his cock. "You'll have to be satisfied with my mouth." She sucked him down again, and this time she didn't mess around. Kenzie fucked him with lips and tongue, finding the rhythm that had pressure building in the base of his spine.

He dug his heels into the mattress, determined to hold out, to make her work for it, but she reached down and cupped his balls, running two fingers toward his ass and pressing just...there.

Liam came so hard he saw stars. Then he saw nothing at

all, his entire world narrowing to the woman kneeling between his thighs, sucking him dry.

He barely waited for his body to recover enough to move before he sat up and toppled her back onto the bed. "Denying me your pussy, Kenzie?"

"We just fucked like five times." She laughed. "I need a little penis break."

"Mmm." He settled between her thighs, loving the way she spread them so readily for him. Brazen, his Kenzie was, and unafraid to demand exactly what she wanted. He pressed an open-mouthed kiss to her pussy. "You're wet, Kenzie. Tells me you liked sucking my cock as much as I did."

He didn't give her a chance to respond before he started fucking her with his tongue. Even after their hours together, she was still so primed for him that she came before he was ready to stop tasting her.

Liam pressed his forehead to her stomach, fighting for control. They needed to sleep. Their bodies needed a goddamn break.

He didn't want to stop.

"The things you do to me."

"Pretty sure it's mutual." She shivered, her voice hoarse. "Why can't I get enough of you?"

Because it's more than sex.

He caught himself before he said the damning words. She recognized it for the truth, she had to, but he knew beyond a shadow of a doubt that Kenzie would bolt if he put a name to the thing growing between them.

He exhaled harshly and sat up. "Come here."

"More cuddling, yay." She grumbled, but she didn't hesitate to tuck herself against him as he laid back down. It felt right to be like this, just like it felt right when he was inside her.

They were still missing some ridiculously large gaps, though.

He smoothed down her hair and pressed a kiss to her temple. "Why is this place called the Island of Ys?"

"Oh, that." She laughed softly. "My sister has a strange sense of humor. It's based on an old French... Myth? Fairytale? Whatever you want to call it."

"I'm not familiar with it." He cuddled her close and pulled the sheets up over them. "Tell it to me."

"You never just ask for things, do you?"

Now it was his turn to laugh. "Please, Kenzie."

"So it goes like this. There was this amazing city—think the French version of Atlantis—and it had these nifty walls that kept the sea at bay. The only way to open said walls was a key the head of the city kept around his neck. Now, this guy was okay, but he had a daughter who was a little too pretty, a little too wild."

"I know someone like that."

"Shh. You wanted a story and now you get it. Don't interrupt." She kissed his chest. "So this daughter fell in love as daughters are inclined to do. Depending on who tells the story, it's just a normal dude or the literal devil. The church really loves their devils. Since love makes fools of us all, she stole the key from her father to meet her lover at the city gates. She unlocked the doors and the water rushed in, drowning both her and the city."

Liam frowned into the darkness. "Not a happy story."

"Depends on if you're the water or the city."

No question which one Kenzie considered herself and the other Horsemen. He ran a hand through her hair, the pieces coming together in a way he hadn't allowed himself to think about until this point. If the Horsemen were the water, then their enemies were the city they surrounded with the intention of bringing down. He'd suspected they had a reason for

97

playing things out a certain way in the Wild Hunt, and though Kenzie hadn't admitted as much, the woman sponsoring the winner *hadn't* left the island.

He opened his mouth, but before he could form words, the phone next to the bed rang. Liam frowned and reached across her to answer. "Yes?"

"Put her on." No misidentifying that icy feminine voice.

He handed the phone to Kenzie. "It's for you."

She took it with a grimace. "Yep?" Kenzie sat straight up. "Okay, I'm on my way. Give me five." She dropped the phone back into its cradle and scrambled off him. "I've got to go."

"What's going on?"

"Can't talk." She marched to the closet and pointed at it. "Open it."

He was losing her. Fuck, but it hadn't been long enough, they hadn't had a chance. "We still have four more days."

"Liam, I would like nothing more than to give you those four days, but this is time sensitive and can't be put off. I *have to go.*" She shoved her hair back. "We'll have those four days when I get back."

If he stood between her and this order, she'd go through him. The truth was written on every line of her body. He held up his hands. "Let me get the key."

"Hurry."

Several seconds later, he fitted the key into the lock and opened the door. "Take me with you."

She hauled her suitcase out onto the floor and pawed through it, coming up with a pair of black leggings and a cropped T-shirt. "What?"

"You're about to put that plan into action. Take me with you."

Kenzie actually hesitated, but finally shook her head. "No. Sorry, but no. This hasn't nothing to do with you." She took one step toward the door and spun around, rushing to press a kiss to his lips. "Thank you." And then she was gone, practically sprinting out the door.

Liam stared after her for a long time. Hurt rose, hardened, became resolve. If Kenzie was leaving the island…

She'd be in danger.

If this woman they took was important enough to orchestrate this level of a revenge scheme, if she was connected to that place that hurt them, then there would be people looking for her. Dangerous people. People who wouldn't hesitate to look down the barrel at Kenzie's beautiful face and pull the trigger.

No. Fuck that.

He would keep her safe.

He just had to figure out how to convince her to let him.

* * *

KENZIE BURST INTO THE HUB, skidding to a stop when she found all her siblings there—and Princess Camilla Fitzcharles. The woman in question stood at Luca's side, her hand in his, and something went sour in Kenzie's stomach. It wasn't jealousy, exactly. She loved Luca and she wanted him to be happy. The princess was more badass than anyone had given her credit for, and Kenzie might even like her if given a chance to hang out.

Damn it, it *was* jealousy.

Jealousy that they had obviously worked out their shit and carved out the possibility of a future together. Jealousy that something in Luca's shoulders seemed lighter, less angry. Jealousy that they were in love.

Get your shit together.

She walked to where Ryu typed furiously on his computer. "What's going on?"

"Declan is here early. He arrived by boat thirty minutes ago."

She frowned. "That's weird. He never deviates from the schedule." Realization washed over her. "He's here for the Bookkeeper. He thinks she might still be on the island."

"Whatever the reason, we can't afford to wait... What the fuck?"

She followed his gaze and turned to find a very familiar face staring up from one of the monitors on the wall. Liam. Kenzie drifted over to stare into those dark eyes, something heavy in her chest. It had been good while it lasted, but all good things had to end. Honestly, it was probably better it ended at a high point, before they went sour. Before he realized she had the kind of issues that made anything resembling a relationship impossible.

A clear and total inability to trust.

The phone rang.

Kenzie frowned at the monitor... Liam had a phone against his ear. She turned just as Amarante answered. "I'm listening." Amarante's brows shot up and then down. "You do know whose island you're currently occupying, don't you, Liam Neale? We could put you out to sea and no one would be the wiser." She listened for several long moments. "I'll consider it." Amarante hung up.

"What the hell was that?" The question came from Luca, who looked furious enough to charge out there and pummel Liam. Or at least attempt to.

Amarante held up a hand, her focus entirely on Kenzie. "Our good friend from the mob has offered his services for the duration of this trip."

"What?" It was like Luca opened his mouth and Kenzie's questions came out.

She pressed her lips together. Apparently Liam had decided his best bet was an attempt to go over her head. She could have told him it was a lost cause. Amarante might head up the Horsemen, but they were a mostly equal partnership. Her sister wouldn't make a call on something like this without her consent.

Sure enough, Amarante crossed her arms over her chest. "He wants to play backup to you, specifically. Apparently, he's concerned about your safety on this trip."

Something warm blossomed in her chest. Liam was worried about her. He wanted to keep her safe. She'd decide later if she was insulted that he thought she couldn't handle it alone. Right now, Kenzie simply luxuriated in the knowledge that someone outside her siblings cared enough to put themselves in danger for her.

She cleared her throat. "And?"

"And what?" Amarante raised a single brow. "It's your call."

Her call. What a novel thought.

Except Kenzie wasn't sure she had enough distance to *make* a call. She looked back at the monitor. Liam stared at the camera so intensely, it was as if he could reach through the digital feed and see her where she stood, as if he knew exactly the thoughts and doubts circling her head.

She could handle this on her own.

She'd done extraction missions before, though usually she was tasked with extracting someone innocent from the bad guys. A special service the Horsemen offered on a limited basis, and only after really intensive checks done by Ryu.

But just because she *could* didn't mean she *should*.

Kenzie glanced at Luca. "You taking the little princess with you?"

"No," he said.

At the same time, Cami said, "Yes."

They glared at each other for a long moment before Luca cursed. "Yes, I'm taking her with."

It might be a good thing to have someone watch her back...

No, Kenzie.

Be honest with yourself if you're not going to be honest with anyone else.

You want him there because you want him close to you.

"I need to talk to him, but if he agrees to my terms, I'll take him with me." She hoped she wasn't making a mistake, but Kenzie couldn't be sure. She didn't quite trust herself where Liam was concerned. For all that, he was more than capable of playing backup. He worked for the most dangerous family in Boston, for fuck's sake. He'd survived some shit, and he would be an asset.

Amarante nodded and moved to lean against Ryu's desk. "You'll have three days. We can keep Declan entertained and running in circles for that long, but eventually even he will realize that he's in danger. You need to have your targets secured by then." She steepled her hands and pressed them to her lips. "The files Ryu put together have everything you need to know, but the true challenge will be timing."

They only had one plane.

She continued. "Luca and the princess will take theirs in Spain first, two days from now. Kenzie, you'll need yours secured and transported to the pickup location fourteen hours after that. Long enough for the plane to land, refuel, and head directly back here." She stared Kenzie down. "We need him alive."

"I'm aware."

"Are you capable of controlling yourself?"

She bristled, but it was a fair question. Kenzie had a history of issues with impulse control, and the man in question had hurt her worse than anyone else. Some days the fantasy of killing him was the only thing that got her through. She closed her eyes and took a deep breath. "I've got this on lock, Te. As long as you promise that, when you're done with him, you let me be the one to end him."

"I promise."

A promise from Amarante was as good as done. She never broke her word. Ever. "Then I promise to bring him back alive." No matter how much she wanted to do otherwise.

Amarante met each of their gazes in turn. "Bring them back. Be safe."

As rousing speeches went, it wasn't top tier, but her sister didn't need rousing speeches to motivate them. After so many years of churning in place, digging deep and creating a safe space for them, they were finally moving forward. It might take time to work their way to the top of the ladder of those responsible for that camp, but they would do it.

They would end their enemy, once and for all.

"The helicopter leaves in an hour. Be ready."

Kenzie wasted no time hauling ass into her suite to shower and pack more appropriate clothing. Her target was in Chicago, which would be significantly colder than their little island paradise. Weapons were next, carefully stored in a locked case. Then there was nothing left but to deal with Liam. She hauled her bags out to the main hub and left them there. Their head of staff, Damien, would take care of transporting them to the helicopter.

Liam had gone back to his room to wait news, and he shoved to his feet when she walked through the door. He frowned. "Your ability to come and go at will leaves a lot to be desired for the security in this place."

"I'm special like that." She held up her hands when he started for her. "No time for that. Here's the deal—you can come with me, on the condition that you follow my orders, don't try any bullshit heroic stuff that will undermine my mission, and follow my orders."

His lips quirked. "You listed follow your orders twice."

"It's the most important rule. If you can't handle that, you're not coming. This is too important to fuck up with some macho bullshit."

He considered her. "And if I think you're in danger?"

"You will follow my orders." He *had* to agree to this. Liam had originally shown every evidence of being a guy who had himself locked down under control, but he'd gone a little feral in the time he'd spent on the island. She had to be sure of him. "Give me your word."

"You trust my word."

She opened her mouth, realized what she'd just said, and shut it. Damn it, maybe she did trust him a little. What the hell was wrong with her? She'd been waiting for revenge for *fifteen years* and she was willing to potentially jeopardize it by bringing along a guy she'd known all of a week.

Not even a week.

"You know what? This was a bad idea. We'll pick this back up—"

"Kenzie, wait." He grabbed her hands. "I'll follow orders. I give my word."

She wanted to believe him. God, how did she get to this point? It would be smarter to leave him behind, to not have that question at her back. Except she didn't want to. "Get your stuff. We're going to Chicago, and it's going to be a quick trip."

He nodded and moved quickly to dig through his suitcase to come up with a duffel bag that he threw clothes into. Liam zipped it up and turned to her. "I don't have any weapons."

"I know." She grinned. "I have enough for both of us."

CHAPTER 10

*T*he second they landed in Chicago, the flirty, brazen Kenzie fell away, leaving someone Liam barely recognized. She was all seriousness as she led the way out of the private hangar to the waiting car. "You drive."

"Sure." He threw their bags in the trunk and climbed into the driver's seat as she programed their destination into the GPS system. Liam waited until they'd traveled off the airport property to ask the question that had been burning since she told him he could accompany her on this trip. "What's the plan?"

He'd read the file she gave him. He knew where Milo was staying, what the guy looked like, the list of crimes he was guilty of. Those alone would be enough to give him a death sentence as far as Liam was concerned. There were lines that couldn't be allowed to be crossed, and hurting children fell squarely in that territory.

This man was the worst child predators had to offer.

Kenzie's voice brought him out of the dark place the file dragged him down to. "We have a hotel overlooking the building where he stays while he's in town. It's locked down pretty tight, but the guy has particular vices that will give me a way in. You take out his men, I tranq the target, we throw him in the trunk and haul ass to the airport. Luca and his princess scoop us up, and then we're back on the island. We have a very small window to make this happen, because we have to time it against Luca's arrival."

He stared so long she frantically motioned for him to keep his eyes on the road. "Kenzie, that kind of op takes weeks to plan, if not months. We don't even have forty-eight hours."

"It's fine. I told you. I have an in."

An in. That could mean absolutely anything, but it sure as fuck sounded like she was about to put herself in this guy's crosshairs. "That's dangerous." He worked to keep his tone mild.

"Yes, it is." She slouched back in the seat. "But with you watching my back, what could go wrong?"

He could list a dozen things off the top of his head. Fuck, but this was a shitty ass plan. Liam kept his mouth shut as they worked their way downtown and finally into the hotel's parking garage. He stayed silent as they checked in and rode the elevator up to the fifteenth floor.

But as soon as he shut the door and flipped the deadbolt, he spun on her. "We'll find another way."

"Liam—"

"Give me a little time, and I'll figure out something."

Kenzie walked up to him. She looked just as divine in her ankle boots, skinny jeans, and thick knitted sweater as she looked in the short dresses she preferred on the island. Better in a way, because she didn't seem quite as untouchable like this. Or maybe that was simply because somewhere along the way, they'd crossed a line with each other that there was no coming back from.

Liam pushed the thought away. He had more important things to focus on right now—namely, her safety.

She stepped into his arms and tangled her fingers in his hair. "We have this covered. I promise."

A promise she had no business making. This plan had more holes in it than a colander. "There has to be a better way."

"There isn't," she said simply. Kenzie pressed a soft kiss to his lips. "Come on. Let's scope this out."

She headed deeper into the suite, and he followed. What else was he supposed to do? If he tried to put his foot down, she'd call his bluff and kick him out. Better that he be here to watch her back as much as he was able. He *would* keep her safe.

Kenzie pulled back the curtains to reveal a view of the street below them and the buildings across the way. "There." She pointed to a wide row of windows directly across and several floors below.

The cocky bastard hadn't even drawn his curtains. It looked like something of a party going on, and Liam took in the women, his heart in his throat. None of them appeared to be children, but that didn't mean they were adults—or there willingly. He couldn't afford to assume anything at this point. "You can't take him out in the middle of a party, Kenzie."

"Yes, thank you, please keep telling me how to do my job." She rolled her eyes. "Today is party city. He only does these things a few times a week. Usually it's just a girl or two for entertainment for him and his guys."

He stared. "Are you trying to comfort me? Because comfort is the last thing I'm feeling right now."

"I'm not trying to comfort you." She turned back to the window. "I can do this alone, Liam. But I would really like you to pull it together to back me up."

Something in her voice, something he really didn't like.

Liam made himself take a mental step back and examine what he knew about her story, this situation, and their target. Realization slammed through him, stealing his breath and leaving only rage in its wake. "Is he one of them?"

"Of course he's one of them. That's why we're here."

He stalked to her. "Is he one of the men who hurt you, specifically?"

Kenzie held her ground. Naturally. The only time she yielded was in the bedroom, and even then it was a struggle. That was different. He didn't want to crowd her, to intimidate her. Liam made himself take a step back, and then another. To give them both space.

She finally sighed. "Yes. Like I said, we never saw anyone's face, but he's got a very distinctive rose tattoo on his neck. I remember that." Her mouth twisted. "I'll never forget that."

She wanted to put herself back in the same room with him.

There was strength and there was insanity. This fell under the latter. "No."

"Excuse me?"

"Absolutely fucking not. It will hurt you to be back in a room with him. *Harm* you. It's not worth it."

Kenzie lifted her chin, her expression smoothing out in a way that spelled trouble. "You don't get to tell me what will or won't harm me. You don't get to tell me this isn't worth it. I am one person, Liam. One single fucking person. Do you know how many kids went through that camp? Because I don't. More than I can count, and most of them didn't last the way we did. They died or they were discarded once they'd been broken beyond compare. That is *still going on*."

"Kenzie—"

"You will let me fucking finish." She didn't raise her voice, but she might as well have taken out a sword and cut him off at the knees. "I am not a saint, and I don't want to go into that room any more than you want me to. But it's a small price to pay to get to the people above him, the ones who put this into motion and continue to enact the kind of evil there are no words for. If you stand in my way, I'll cut you down, too."

* * *

LIAM LEFT the hotel room after she drew her line in the sand, and part of Kenzie hoped he was gone for good. Or at least that was what she told herself as she settled in to watch her target. Milo had a woman under each arm, a cigarette in one hand, and a bottle of beer in the other. On the table in front of him, one of his men created several little white lines.

How the fuck was he still alive if he'd spent the last fifteen years partying like this?

She pushed to her feet and glanced at the door. It would be better if Liam had washed his hands of her. He hadn't exactly looked at her differently after she'd told him some of what went down in that camp, but eventually he would. Once he saw the scars left over. She'd been luckier than Luca in that way—all Kenzie's scars were internal. The few times one of the patrons hurt her badly enough to wound, she'd received the best medical care and they'd gone above and beyond in their attempt to keep her beauty from being marred.

A pretty doll to be used as they saw fit.

To be used as Milo saw fit.

She turned away from the window. She couldn't stand to look at him any longer. Maybe she should have taken Arthur and sent Luca and the princess here instead. Her brother carried his own baggage—they all did—but he wouldn't be in danger of putting a bullet between Milo and leaving it at that.

Probably.

She sighed. Tomorrow they'd have to meet with the guy Ryu found who supplied the girls Milo played with, and sometimes broke. She could theoretically broker the deal herself, playing the part of a naive small-town girl who thought the only thing she was signing up for was to give some rich dude a girlfriend experience. It would be easier to pull off with Liam, though.

She hadn't quite gotten around to telling him that part of the plan yet, because she knew exactly what he'd say.

The door opened and Kenzie jumped. Liam walked in with two white plastic takeout bags. He raised his eyebrows at her, all of the earlier anger and frustration gone. "We're going to eat, and then you're going to go over every detail of the plan."

"Actually—"

"If I'm satisfied, then we'll move forward with it."

Kenzie blinked. "You want to run that by me again?"

He strode to the small table behind the couch and set the food there. "Come here."

"Okay…" She moved to him slowly, taking in the way the lines on his face seemed a little deeper than they had been when he first arrived on the island. Part of that came from the Wild Hunt, but she had no illusions who held the blame for the rest.

Her.

"Why do you bother, Liam? I'm sure there are other women in Boston—or, hell, the world—who wouldn't put you through the wringer and don't have a boatload worth of baggage that requires stalking and kidnapping people." Women who could love him with their whole hearts instead of the sum of all its broken pieces.

Loving someone back to wholeness might work in romance novels, but real life was significantly messier. Kenzie wasn't whole. She wasn't sure she ever had been. Even with a lifetime of therapy, she'd never be a woman who worked well as a civilian. Not when she knew how deep the rot ran beneath the surface of this world. As one of the Horsemen, as War, she was in a position to do something about it.

More importantly in some ways, she was free of having to cram herself into a box to make other people more comfortable.

Liam looked down at her for a long time and then held out his hand. "Come here," he repeated softly.

She shouldn't. This thing between them had an expiration date and the second she stopped fighting getting close to him was the second she lost something more valuable than any bet.

But Kenzie was so damn tired of standing alone. She had her siblings, yes, and she leaned on them heavily at times, but it felt different with Liam. She slipped her hand into his and allowed him to pull her slowly into his arms.

"Maybe there are other women. World is more than half women at this point. Maybe I could try to find someone who would suit." He hugged her tightly, big arms wrapping around her, anchoring her to the here and now. "I don't want them, Kenzie. I never wanted them. I knew from the moment I saw you that this was meant to be something, and I'll keep fighting until you believe it, too."

She pressed her face to his shirt and inhaled. He smelled good, though she couldn't begin to label the notes of his scent. It was simply Liam. "That kind of connection only exists in fiction."

"And yet here we are."

Hard to argue that. Especially considering the lengths

he'd gone through to find her again. She finally lifted her head. "You know, if I was anyone else, I might decide that you're a creepy stalker who I need a restraining order against."

His lips curved. "Are there restraining orders on the island?"

"No. There's just Death." She made a face. "Or I guess Famine is the one who would kick your ass to the curb. My sister prefers to keep her interactions with the general population to a bare minimum."

"I see." He kept one arm around her waist and smoothed back her hair with his free hand. "I like you, Kenzie."

Her heartbeat kicked up roughly a thousand notches. "I... like you, too."

Liam nodded as if he hadn't expected any different. He pressed a quick kiss to her lips and released her. "Let's go over the plan."

Right. The plan.

Dazed, she sank onto the couch and watched Liam lay out the food. "My brother dug up a contact who finds the girls Milo uses, both for the big parties and the private ones. I need you to broker the deal, either as the guy selling me or as my boyfriend looking to make a quick buck."

His hand froze in the middle of opening the second bag. "You want me to sell you to that man."

It wasn't quite a question. Kenzie cleared her throat. "I can do it if you're not comfortable with that. It's not as common, but I can play naive co-ed easily enough." She'd done it before, though she wasn't about to tell Liam that. Not with the flat way he looked at her as if considering tying her up and tossing her in a closet until he found a way to do this without endangering her.

It felt...weirdly nice that he cared about whether this

would hurt her or not. Because that's what it was. He didn't protest this because he thought she couldn't handle it. He didn't want her to have to face this particular demon from her past. "Liam, it's okay."

"It's not okay, but I'm dealing with it." He finished setting out the food—Chinese—and waited for her to choose what she wanted before he grabbed one of the other cartons. "How do we get him out of the apartment?"

She breathed a silent sigh of relief. "He parties hard, so I'm going to dose him with a sedative that will leave him looking like he's drank his weight in alcohol. Still able to sort of walk with our help, but not coherent enough to remember anything or even speak."

Liam took a bite and chewed slowly. "Walk me through it."

"Ryu's contact will take me and probably another girl or two up to the apartment. I'll have to play it by ear because Milo never has fewer than three guys with him at all times. They're paid muscle and even if I'm better than they are, four against one isn't the greatest of odds."

He nodded. "Agreed."

"I'll try to dose his drink, but it'll depend on how things play out." If she had to, she'd shove the drugs right down that fucker's throat. "The goal is to sedate him, let you into the hotel room, and the two of us will take care of the muscle. The girls we'll pay off and kick out. Then we walk Milo right out the back door. Luca will meet us at the airport, we pop him on the plane, and then we're on our way back to the Island of Ys."

"There are half a dozen things that can go wrong with every single step of that plan."

Kenzie shrugged a single shoulder. "There are usually a lot of things that can go wrong with any plan." He had a point, though. They should have had another week to get the details finessed on this, but Declan showing up early put everything on a rush. She didn't like that, didn't like what it might mean. "We're working with what we have."

He finally nodded. "I need a key for that apartment."

"They're coded for fingerprints, rather than actual keys."

"Can your brother hack it?"

"Hold that thought." She went and grabbed her phone and came back. Kenzie dialed Ryu's number and put it on speaker.

"Yeah?"

"Can you hack the door in Milo's apartment?"

Anyone else would have asked questions, required verification. Not Ryu. "It's a closed-circuit lock that requires fingerprints."

Liam leaned forward. "What about the manager? Someone must be able to get in for maintenance."

"Give me a few." Furious clicking was the only sound as Ryu followed the information. It made her dizzy to watch when he did it with her in the room. How someone could keep track of three screens while typing so fast was beyond Kenzie. She could work a computer just fine, but her brother was magic when it came to tech stuff.

Finally, the clicking stopped. "There's an override code in case of emergency. It'll take me a little time to get access to it, but I'll forward the information when I do."

"Thanks."

"Be safe."

"You, too." She hung up and sat back. "Okay, fine. That was a good idea."

Liam gave her a tight smile. "I'm not without my merits."

No one in their right mind would say that Liam was without merits. She couldn't have tailor-made someone better suited to move through her world if she'd tried. But then, she and Liam's worlds overlapped more than a little. She'd be a fool to forget that, to overlook where he'd come from and who he worked for.

Kenzie worked really hard not to be a fool.

She wasn't about to start now.

CHAPTER 11

"*D*o you ever regret the things you've done?"

The question caught Liam off-guard. He sat back and really looked at Kenzie, taking in the tired drop in her shoulders, the way she kept her expression carefully blank. The question seemed innocent enough, but it was loaded in a thousand different ways. "No."

She blinked. "Just that. No?"

"I can't afford regret. If I regret, that means I might hesitate to do what's necessary the next time conflict rolls around. There are things I would go back and do differently, I suppose, but at the end of the day I'm simply following orders."

"That's very...soldier of you. Following orders so the guilt falls on the one giving them."

He hadn't exactly thought about it that way. "It's not so simple as that." When Kenzie seemed unconvinced, he tried to elaborate. "There are rules in my world. Not everyone plays by them, but the O'Malleys do. We don't fuck around with people who aren't moving on the same spectrum that we do, which means I'm never sent after someone who isn't guilty of all sorts of shit. It makes it easier to sleep at night."

"You've never hurt someone who isn't playing by the same rules as you?"

He thought back, though Liam already knew the answer. "Not that I'm aware of."

"Wow." She blew out a breath. "That's weirdly honorable of you, considering you're attached to the freaking Irish mob."

"Throwing stones, Kenzie?"

She laughed. "No, of course not. Sometimes it just surprises me how alike we are."

Alike.

Such a fragile word for the soul-deep connection Liam felt with her. It should have freaked him the fuck out. His world was a carefully balanced one with a specific order. When he sought out Kenzie, he hadn't realized she *was* Kenzie. He thought he could somehow have both—the woman he couldn't forget and the only life he'd always known. With each day, each hour, he spent with her, he couldn't shake the knowledge that at some point he'd have to choose.

Kenzie or the O'Malleys.

Fuck, but he hadn't prepared for that.

Liam pushed it away. He had to set it aside. In the next forty-eight hours, he would be playing backup to Kenzie and extracting a monster. Nothing needed to be decided now, and he couldn't afford to be distracted in the meantime. If he missed a step because he was too worried about what the future might hold, he ran the risk of her being hurt.

He ran the risk of losing her in the most permanent of ways.

Fear flared, cold and cloying, digging into his lungs and

heart and stomach. A world without Kenzie was unacceptable. He shoved to his feet and rounded the table to her. "I need you."

She frowned, but let him pull her to her feet. "Are you okay?"

"No." He pulled her sweater off and urged her to shimmy out of her jeans. As tempting as it was to set her on the table and fuck her right here, he needed something beyond the bliss of orgasm. He needed to lose himself completely in her. To ground himself. Liam picked her up and strode through the doorway into the bedroom. The bed was just as luxurious as the rest of the suite, something he might appreciate if he could put on the brakes for half a second.

A lost cause, that.

Liam laid Kenzie down on the bed and then crawled up to join her. She pulled him down to her, wrapping her long legs around his waist. "Tell me what you need."

"You. I need you, Kenzie. Just you."

She hesitated for the breadth of a second and then everything about her went soft. She cupped his face between her hands and ran her thumbs along his cheekbones. "I don't know what to do with you," she whispered. "Every time I think I know what you want, you change the game."

"This isn't a game." He turned his head and kissed one of her palms and then the other. "No power plays. No commands and obedience. No masks. Just Kenzie. Just Liam. Just...us."

"I don't know if I can be just Kenzie." She gave a sad smile. "I'm a shark, Liam. I have to keep swimming or I'm going to drown."

"I'll keep you afloat." He brushed his lips against hers, silently requesting access. She parted for him on a sigh, and Liam slipped his tongue into her mouth. Searching for something that had no name. Kenzie met him halfway. She *always* met him halfway. Something he loved about her. The woman had never met a line she wasn't willing to step to—and over.

Her hands slid from his face down his chest and around to his back, holding him close even as she kept matching his slow, drugging kisses. He rocked against her without meaning to, his cock sliding against her, spreading her wetness.

Always ready, his Kenzie.

Liam lost himself in the pleasure of her body moving against him. The slide of her soft skin again his. Her nails lightly digging into his back as he rocked his hips again, sliding the length of his cock against her clit. Again and again, spinning a spell of pleasure around them that he never wanted to end. Better to stay in this moment where nothing could hurt them, where the desire and emotion sparking along his nerve endings made time stretch in strange ways.

I want this forever.

I want you *forever.*

Words he couldn't say, not without ruining things between them. Instead, Liam was determined to show her. He rolled his hips again, loving the way her thighs tightened around him as she moaned against his lips. "God, Liam, not-fucking shouldn't feel so damn good."

"It should when it's us." He dragged his mouth down her neck and flicked his tongue against the hollow of her throat. "You make me crazy."

"The feeling is entirely mutual."

He slid his hands between her and the bed, holding them tighter together. "Tell me yes, Kenzie."

"What?" She let loose a breathless laugh. "Baby, I'm practically begging for your cock right now—for you. It's not a yes, it's a *hell yes.*" She dug her ankles into the small of his back, urging him closer yet. "Fuck me, Liam. Hard and rough and until the only thing I'm capable of doing is screaming your name."

"I love it when you do that." He nipped her bottom lip and moved back just enough for his cock to drop down to her entrance. "You have such a filthy mouth. It gets me so fucking hot to see those pretty red lips telling me all the things you want me to do to you."

She moaned as he slid fully into her, and Liam pressed his forehead to hers, fighting for control. As much as he wanted to follow through on the promise of fucking her, he needed this too.

They both did.

Slowly, oh so achingly slowly, he withdrew and eased back into her. Torturing. Teasing. It was nowhere near the rough fucking she wanted, but that didn't stop Kenzie from kissing his neck and jaw, working her way back to his mouth. "You're evil."

"You love it."

She grinned against his lips. "Maybe."

And then there was no more space for talking. Words simply couldn't compare to the way her breath caught. To the growl in the back of his throat he couldn't quite smother. To the way their bodies moved in perfect unison. She was perfect. Everything about this was perfect.

He wedged his arm beneath the small of her back, lifting her hips to get the angle they both needed. The one that would drive her over the edge and have her coming around his cock. Kenzie let her arms fall over her head, mimicking the position she'd had not so long ago in his bed on the island. This time there was no headboard to hold onto. Her breasts shook with each long thrust and she moaned, her hands clenching the sheets. "There. Right there."

Liam forced himself to hold the position, the rhythm, to

give her everything she needed even as she went wild around him. Kenzie came with a cry, and hell if he wouldn't sell his soul to hear his name on her lips in exactly that tone for the rest of his life.

Too bad that bargain had already been made.

Eight years ago in a hotel room not too different from this one.

Kenzie had taken a piece of him that night, and he couldn't shake the feeling that she took the rest tonight as he drove into her and came with a curse. Liam had no regrets. She saw him in a way that few people did.

If she wanted his bruised soul, he would hand it over gladly.

* * *

FOR THE FIRST time in her adult life, Kenzie didn't know what came next. Ever since they'd bought the Island of Ys and put it together from the ground up, she'd had a direction to point herself. She *still* had a direction when it came to vengeance. But in all that, she'd never really thought about what the future would look like for her personally.

She wasn't sure she could afford to think about it now.

She coasted her hand over Liam's chest. "I don't know how to do this thing you want to do."

"What thing I want to do?"

"You know. The relationship thing. You didn't go through all this just to fuck me, though I think we can both agree that I'm worth it."

Liam's chuckle rumbled through his chest. "Yes, Kenzie. You're worth it." He cuddled her closer and pressed a kiss to the top of her head. "To be honest, I don't know how to do 'the relationship thing' either."

At that, she lifted her head, sure he was screwing with

her. Liam must have been in relationships before now. He was so...Liam. Before he'd come to the island, he was the very picture of strong and steady, and there was absolutely no way women didn't flock to that, even with the mob ties. Maybe even *because* of the mob ties. "Funny."

"I'm serious." No mirth in his dark eyes. "Why do you think it took me so long to come looking for you?"

"Because you had to exhaust your resources before you realized that I couldn't be found."

His lips quirked at that. "Valid point, but ultimately a side effect to the larger reason. I was... I *am*...One of the O'Malley family's men. There was never any question of that when I was a kid, and by the time Aiden and I became friends, that was my path." He gently urged her head back to his chest and pulled the sheets over them. "And, yes, there were women when I was in my twenties, but I kept the dating casual because I was working up the ranks and my focus had to be there. By the time Aiden was poised to take over for his father, I'd already been ruined."

"Ruined." She frowned.

"Yeah. I met this gorgeous blond who blew my mind and took my wallet, and after that, no other woman could really compare."

At that, she sat up. "You have *not* spent eight years celibate."

"Fuck, no."

Kenzie exhaled a sigh of relief. He already put so much pressure on this thing, for the sole reason that Liam had gone through so much effort to find her again. She toyed with a strand of her hair, hating how vulnerable this conversation made her feel. Vulnerability Liam didn't seem to blink at. It didn't make him weak to admit he'd wanted her, had chased her across the years and half the world.

Maybe it was time to do some admitting of her own.

She couldn't quite make herself meet his gaze. "I kept track of you...for a little while."

"You did?" Next to her, Liam didn't seem to draw breath.

"For a year or two. It was kind of a similar situation. We'd just opened the Island of Ys and the big focus was drawing in the right kind of people. It took all four of us working overtime to make it happen, and the opportunity to make another stop in Boston never came up. But, yeah, you made an impression on me. I looked you up every few months at first, but the more time that passed, the harder it was to look back. Eventually, I stopped looking altogether."

He touched her chin, guiding her back to face him. "You said you didn't remember until I forced the issue. You looked at me with absolutely no recognition during the Wild Hunt."

"You don't live through what I've lived through without developing some troubling coping mechanisms. All my siblings deal in their own ways, but I learned to forget. I can't afford to forget everything. It would paint a target on my forehead and make me worse than useless. But I forget the memories that threaten to cripple me. I have to."

He looked at her for a long time. "The memory of me threatened to cripple you."

No question there, but she had to answer it nonetheless. "It was too good," Kenzie whispered. "One night shouldn't be good enough to make me reconsider things I knew for truth. Like you, I couldn't afford to be distracted. Too much hung in the balance—*still* hangs in the balance." She couldn't ride off into the sunset with this man. There was no happily ever after in Kenzie's future, especially not now when they were so close to figuring out who actually ran Camp Bueller. Her siblings needed her head in the game, and here she was, naked and tangled up in Liam.

She started to edge off the bed. "I should get dressed."

"Wait." Liam sat up. "You know I wouldn't keep you from the plot you four are spinning out. There are lines, Kenzie, and what those people did more than crossed them. They deserve to be put down." He bracketed her wrist with one of his big hands and tugged her back toward him. "But that doesn't mean you have to stop living."

"You think I've stopped living?" Her laugh came out half-hearted at best. "I live the fullest out of everyone."

"Maybe." He didn't stop until she was sprawled on his chest. "Or maybe that's another way of forgetting."

How dare this man use his words to crack open the very heart of her?

Kenzie tried and failed to dredge up any righteous anger. "I can't do this."

"Why?"

One word.

A single word to send her protests crumbling down around her. She pressed her lips together and closed her eyes, striving for control, for something she had no name for. "You distract me, Liam. Can you imagine trying to navigate the turf wars the O'Malleys almost started a few years back if you had me waiting at home for you?"

His laugh surprised her so much, she opened her eyes. Liam rolled them, pinning her to the bed even as he grinned down at her. "In what universe would you be the little wife waiting at home? We both know damn well that you'd have my back on any battleground I walked onto."

She stared up at him. "I'm going to need you to say that again."

"Kenzie, is it really so hard to believe that I *see* you? That I accept all the parts of you that make up the whole?"

Yes. Yes, it was really that hard to believe. The only people who truly accepted her were her siblings, and none of them wanted to fuck her. And the only people who *did* want to fuck her… that's all they wanted. They saw what she let them see and they accepted it as fact. No one bothered to dig beneath the surface level to find out what lay beneath. Up until this point, she'd been content with that. She didn't *want* to be exposed to someone who could rip her heart out and toss it in the trash when they were finished with her.

Every single lesson she'd learned to survive centered around protecting herself because once people accomplished their goals and no longer found her useful, they would always walk away, not caring if they left her broken and bleeding behind them.

She couldn't afford to believe that Liam was the exception to the rule. It would hurt too much when he walked away.

And he *would* walk away. No matter what he might or might not feel for her, everyone he cared about was in Boston. *His life* was in Boston. It might take time, but eventually he'd tire of dancing around her issues and chasing her demons, and then he'd go home. The O'Malleys finally had peace, and all Kenzie had to offer him was war.

She didn't know what showed on her face, but Liam frowned. "Don't banish me from the island when we get back. Give me time to prove that I mean what I say."

Did she dare?

"I can't promise anything," Kenzie whispered. Not more time on the island, not a future, not her heart.

Frustration rolled through his expression, but he finally gave a short nod. "Then we'll talk about it when we get back."

A reprieve, and not a long one at that. Relief cascaded through her all the same. "Okay."

Liam's mouth tightened as if he'd seen the relief and didn't like it, but he dipped down and kissed her before she could decide how she felt about that. Kenzie let herself sink into the feeling of his mouth on hers, let the taste of him chase away her fears.

This, she understood. *This*, she could deal with.

Just because she craved him like her next breath didn't mean he would break her heart.

Not when Kenzie didn't think she even had a heart left to break.

CHAPTER 12

*K*enzie stayed in bed with Liam most of the day, taking regular breaks to keep tabs on Milo. He never left his apartment, but why would he? Everything he needed was delivered right to his door. Ryu had said he was in Chicago for some kind of deal that was supposed to go down next week, but she couldn't care less since it didn't seem to have anything to do with Camp Bueller.

Why would it?

That camp disappeared fifteen years ago. Surely a new one had risen up to replace it, but Milo had only ever come once a month or so to slake his needs.

Kenzie shuddered.

No.

She refused to go down that twisted little memory lane. She certainly couldn't afford to think about whatever little blond girl replaced Kenzie in the next camp or the things he'd have done to his new plaything. His new *doll*.

Bile rose, acid eating away at her defenses. She shoved the blankets off her. "I need a shower."

"Kenzie—"

The concern in Liam's voice was nearly her undoing. "I'm fine. I just need… I just need a few minutes." She could feel his gaze on her as she strode away from the bed and into the bathroom. After a quick battle with herself, she shut and locked the door. It was a dead giveaway to the fact that she was most assuredly not okay, but better to keep Liam out than to let him witness the ugly things bubbling up inside her.

Kenzie scrambled to turn on the shower, cranking it as hot as it could go. Her stomach lurched again, and she had one horrified moment wondering if she'd actually be sick. When was the last time she puked? She couldn't even remember. She might indulge to excess in a number of ways, but she never fully lost control.

Or at least she hadn't until this week.

A slow breath. Another. Again and again, until she muscled past the need to expel her lunch. She stepped beneath the spray and flinched at the heat. Each point of stinging pain drove back the memories, washed away the old certainty that she'd never be clean.

She knew better now.

He'd hurt her. He'd wanted to break her in ways that tattooed his name across her very soul.

But he failed.

She braced her hands on the tile and let the water pour over her as she pieced herself back together again. It had been so long since she'd had to do this, years maybe. For better or worse, Kenzie was a survivor and that meant facing down her past until she could move forward. Wasn't that what they were doing right now? Putting their demons to bed once and for all.

That was all she needed to focus on.

The mission.

Get the bastard. Bring him back to the island.

Amarante would take out punishment for his sins in blood and pain, and she'd get answers in the process. It was her gift, after all. One *they* forced on her, the same way they dressed Kenzie up like a living doll and handed her to whoever paid the right price.

Damn it, she was doing a terrible job of getting her head on straight.

She twisted the water handle, changing the temperature to freezing. The blast shocked a curse from her lips, and she could finally *think*.

This was a mistake.

I should have given Milo to Luca.

She took one last deep breath and shut off the water. This particular trick hadn't succeeded. Maybe she could sweat some of this horrible feeling off, though somehow she doubted Liam would fight her again, and fucking was out of the question. Kenzie dried off quickly and opened the door.

Liam sat on the corner of the bed with a direct line of sight to the bathroom, his expression carefully closed down. "What can I do?"

Just that.

No demand for answers or details. No needing her to trot out her past in order to convey the living nightmare surging beneath her skin.

Just simple understanding.

She cleared her throat. The mission. They had to focus on the mission. "How long until the meet tonight?"

He didn't look at the clock. "Four hours."

Enough time. It had to be enough. Kenzie bounced on her toes, her body too filled with nervous energy to stay still. "Spar with me?"

"Spar." His attention sharpened on her. "Are you looking to hurt or be hurt?"

There were times when she found his perceptiveness

incredibly aggravating. This moment didn't number among them. "Both," she whispered.

He could have argued with her. She half expected him to. *Normal* people didn't need to beat down their pain physically. If she was back on the island, she'd throw together one of her famed matches. There was always someone around who wanted a chance to take her down a notch—and always a crowd of people happy to bet on it. In a pinch one of her brothers would step in for a private sparring session.

Never Amarante, though.

Amarante didn't spar. When she fought, she wasn't capable of pulling her punches.

Liam pushed slowly to his feet. "Get dressed. I'll find us a place."

Was this what love felt like? This balloon in her chest that hurt and soothed at the same time? She wanted to throw herself into his arms, but she needed this fight more than she needed to be held.

Maybe the holding could come later...

She dressed quickly, and by the time she laced up her shoes, Liam reappeared, clothed in workout shorts and a sweatshirt. "I found a gym."

"A gym." She hesitated. "We don't have to—"

"Kenzie." He picked up her jacket and handed it to her. "If you need this, then we're going to do it right. Come on."

And that was all there was left to say.

Twenty minutes later, he led her through a dingy looking door and into a gym that would have been perfectly at home in a *Rocky* movie. Old and worn down and smelling faintly of sweat, but with a history that she could feel through the soles of her shoes. *This is the place.*

"Warm up." Liam nodded at the punching bag in the corner and then headed toward the pair of grizzled old black guys sitting in a chair next to the ring. There was only one other guy in the place, a muscle-bound white guy with headphones in who went after one of the giant punching bags like it owed him money.

Kenzie made her way to the corner where Liam had directed her. She took her first full breath in an hour and went through her warmup. It felt good. Really good. By the time her body was loose and fluid, she felt almost like herself again.

Almost.

Liam must have been watching her because he walked up just as she finished her last exercise. He'd lost his shirt somewhere along the way, and he'd wrapped his hands in tape. He motioned and she reluctantly set her hands in his and allowed him to tape her up as well. "I'd rather not," Kenzie said.

"I know." He didn't stop the smooth movements. He'd definitely done this before. "But we have tonight to think of."

Tonight.

When she would willingly walk into that room and have to smile for the monster who put so many scars on her soul.

Just like that, the sliver of hard-won calm disappeared. She gritted her teeth and forced herself to stillness while Liam finished up on her hands. Bouncing might feel better, but it would prolong the wait to get into the ring.

He squeezed her hands. "Three rounds."

"Liam—"

"Three rounds, Kenzie. I'll make sure you get what you need."

How could he, when the thing she needed most was against Amarante's direct orders? For what felt like the millionth time, she cursed her arrogance in picking Milo as her target.

She climbed into the ring and gave into the restless energy demanding she bob and weave. On the other side,

Liam was pool of stillness. Out of habit, she took him in as an opponent.

He'd hurt his leg in the Wild Hunt. Not bad enough to affect his mobility in the weeks since, but she suspected it was a weak point she could exploit. When he moved, though, he was just as fluid as she was. "You've spent time in the ring before." She'd noticed it during their last bout, but she was more focused on the endgame—on getting into his pants—to think too hard about it.

"A long time ago." A ghost of a smile on his lips. "I had anger issues in my early twenties."

If she hadn't seen how he was in the bedroom, she might not have believed that dry statement. For all Liam's control, he had a well of rage nearly as deep as hers. It called to her, flame to flame. "Ready?"

"Yes."

They circled each other, their fists up. Liam seemed content to wait her out, but patience had never been Kenzie's strong suit. She struck first, feinting left and then right to get a better read on him. Again and again, drawing them closer. Still, he didn't attack.

"Stop stalling," she hissed.

Conflict flared in Liam's gaze for the briefest of seconds. She thought she'd have to bait him, but he moved before she had a chance. Liam swung at her face, surprising her so much she barely ducked in time.

And then the bastard swept her legs out from beneath her.

Kenzie landed on her back and rolled, springing to her feet with a curse. "You're holding back."

"So are you."

Damn it, but he was right. She wouldn't get through this unless they both dialed it in.

Kenzie stopped messing around. She took a breath and

then she went at Liam. She was smaller and his range was significantly longer, but she suspected he would keep holding back until she forced him not to.

She feinted a left hook and then punched him in the stomach. Liam bent over with a rasped curse, but he caught her kick before her foot made contact with his face. When he looked up at her with those dark eyes, she almost laughed in relief. He wasn't playing any longer.

Thank fuck.

She danced back, letting him catch his breath. It didn't take long. Liam came after her on quick feet. Round and round, they circled the ring, trading punches. She got him in the side. He returned the favor of knocking her breath from her body. Again and again.

He never touched her face.

She stayed away from his recovering leg.

Finally Liam tackled her, taking them both to the ground. Sweat slicked their bodies and they were both breathing hard. He stared down at her, letting the weight of his body hold her in place. "You good?"

She started to make a smart-ass comment, but stopped. This wasn't small talk. He was checking in. She owed an honest answer in response. "I don't think I'll be good until we're back on the island, but I'm not going out of my skin anymore."

"Let's go." He climbed off her and pulled her to her feet.

A quick glance at the faded clock on the wall told her it'd been twenty minutes. A hell of a long time for a fight, but she suspected Liam had drawn it out on purpose to bleed off the worst of the toxic feeling driving her.

They walked back to the hotel in silence. Half a dozen times, Kenzie opened her mouth to explain. Half a dozen times, the words wouldn't form. In the face of her glaring weakness, she had nothing to offer him. She couldn't promise that this would never happen again, because it *did* happen from time to time. Less and less as the years went on, but she didn't think it'd ever go away.

Back in their room, Liam took her hand and towed her into the bathroom. Kenzie let him strip her, amazed that this man who could be so sexual chose to keep it dialed back this time. She wouldn't be opposed to fucking in the shower but...

He was right. It wasn't what she needed right now.

It felt good to let Liam take care of her, to relax into his hands sliding over her skin as he washed her body and then his. By the time they stepped out of the shower, Kenzie almost felt like herself again.

"Thank you."

Liam wrapped her in a towel and pulled her close, hugging her tightly to him. "You have nothing to thank me for."

"Yes, I do." She leaned into him and rested her head on his chest. "Just...thank you."

"You don't have to do this. We can find another way."

She wished that was true, but Kenzie had never run from a fight before, and she wasn't about to start with the most important one. "This is bigger than me and my...fear." Yes, fear. That was the feeling sending her spiraling again and again when she thought about tonight. "There's no one else who can do this."

"Kill him."

"What if he's the one with the information we need? Three people isn't that many in the grand scheme of things. It's possible that they each have a piece to the whole. Or that something will go wrong with one of the others. We can't risk it." She reached up and ran her hand along Liam's jaw. "He'll pay. Trust me on that if you trust me on nothing else.

Death will take out his penance in blood, and then I'll finish what's left of him."

His brows lowered. "Your sister is freaky as shit."

"We both are." She gave a sad smile. "We all do what we have to in order to keep the past from nipping at our heels. Amarante is no different."

"Amarante." He spoke her name slowly, understanding written across his face. "Thank you for trusting me with her name."

"I trusted you with mine first." She went on tip toes and kissed him softly. "I need to get ready."

"If you change your mind—"

"I won't."

Liam ignored her. "If you change your mind at any point, I'll get you out. If that means I have to face down Amarante in the process, so be it."

Kenzie laughed. She couldn't help it. "My sister would kill you."

"She'd try."

She stepped out of his arms and bent over to wrap her towel around her head. "No, Liam. She wouldn't try. She'd kill you. You are a hard ass who's done what you need to do your entire life. Yes, you have a kill count, but I imagine most of them weren't personal. Not the kind of personal that drives a person slowly to the ledge and over it." She straightened and turned to the mirror where she had arranged all her cosmetics. "Every time Amarante kills, it's like that. She takes it all personally, and she goes after everyone who stands in her way as if they keep her from the one thing she wants most."

Liam hooked his towel around his waist and leaned against the door frame, seeming content to watch her get ready. It was...strangely domestic. The only people who'd ever seen her go through this ritual were her siblings, and most of the time they almost felt like an extension of Kenzie herself. Family.

He crossed his arms over his chest. "What about the other one—Pestilence?"

"Ryu."

He didn't blink. "He's the computer guy."

"He's the backbone of this entire thing," she corrected as she went to work with primer on her skin. She didn't use it most of the time on the island, but there were faint circles under her eyes, and she looked exhausted. Not the kind of girl their contact would want to send up to Milo. No, she had to be flawless—or at least appear that way. "Ryu and Amarante are blood siblings. They were in that camp longer that either me or Luca. A lot longer. Ryu is the one who used his affinity with computers to get us the funding we needed for the island."

It had taken him years to get that good. Years of them doing small time hustles and pickpocketing in order to survive. Years when there were times she got so hungry, she actually considered bargaining her body again. Even if it would break her. Better broken than starving.

Amarante wouldn't hear of it. Every time it got that bad, every time Kenzie brought up that option, Amarante would disappear for several hours and when she came back, she'd bring enough food to last them days.

Kenzie still didn't know what her sister had done to accomplish that.

"Luca is Famine," Liam mused. "He's a dick."

"He's overprotective." Truth be told, they all were.

Liam watched her apply her contouring and eye shadow. "Family is complicated."

"Yes." She carefully blended the browns of the eyeshadow into a subtle smoky eye look. Intense enough to pass for evening, but a more natural version of it. "You would know."

"Only by proxy. The O'Malleys are..." He gave a small smile. "Complicated. Aiden might be my best friend, but there's a power dynamic there that neither of us can escape. I will never be family, and so we'll never quite be equal."

She paused and met his gaze in the mirror. "He cares about you. That's not a lie."

"No, it's not a lie. We're friends. We'll just never..." Liam shook his head. "This is stupid. I have a good life. Yeah, I skate on the wrong side of the law, but it's a good life."

He sounded like he was trying to convince himself more than her. "But?"

"But there's something missing, and I can't—won't settle until I've found that missing piece." He deliberately turned away and walked into the room.

Her.

He was talking about *her*.

The fluttering in her stomach had nothing to do with what came later that night and everything to do with the realization that Liam wasn't going to walk after their allotted time was up. For better or worse, he'd set his sights on her and he'd stay until she was forced to make a decision.

Kenzie took a slow breath to steady the hand holding her mascara wand. She didn't know what the future held. She *couldn't* think about it now, not with what came next hanging over her head.

But maybe...

Maybe they could find a way.

Maybe.

CHAPTER 13

*L*iam did *not* want to send Kenzie alone with the skeezy motherfucker who would deliver her to Milo. The man didn't *look* skeezy, naturally. He was a thin Mexican guy who wore a suit and smiled charmingly at Kenzie in a way designed to disarm. It might have worked if Liam couldn't practically see him adding up the bonus he'd get for delivering her to that suite upstairs.

She'd dressed to impress tonight, and it showed. Her tight black dress barely covered the essentials, leaving her breasts pressing against the top as if one deep breath would show nipple and the lower curve of her ass flashing every time she bent the slightest bit forward. Her sky-high heels made the most of her legs and her blond hair was styled in a way that looked like she'd just been thoroughly fucked.

He was torn between wanting to drag her to some shady corner and show her how much he appreciated the look and wanting to wrap her in his coat and bundle her away from this club and this city and this fucking country.

Their contact, Marco, gave Kenzie another smile. "Be a good girl and go get us a drink." He pressed cash into her hand, missing the way her amber eyes flared in fury before she masked the response.

The slip in her mask worried Liam more than anything else. She was smiling and flirting and acting the part of a clueless pretty girl, but he knew her well enough by now to see the underlying tension.

Kenzie was in danger of shattering.

Again, Liam cursed himself for not finding a way around this. She'd never forgive him if he stepped in and took care of that piece of shit they needed to extract. Kenzie wouldn't see it as him saving her. Liam would become an obstacle, and he already knew how Kenzie—how the Horsemen—dealt with obstacles.

In trying to protect her, he'd lose her forever.

As soon as she bounced off to the bar, Marco turned to Liam. "I'll give you twenty grand for her."

It took every ounce of self-control to keep his rage off his face. As if Kenzie was worth such a pittance. As if she wasn't fucking *priceless*. He raised his brows. "We both know your guy would pay a hundred for her without blinking. She's prime cut, so don't fuck with me."

Marco studied him as if trying to gauge whether he was bluffing or not. "She better be worth the promise that ass makes for that kind of money."

"She's worth more." That, at least, was the truth.

Another beat of hesitation and Marco shrugged. "Sure, man. Just don't expect her to thank you for this. My man doesn't break his toys as often as he used to, but it happens."

Christ.

"He breaks her, I come looking for you."

Marco held up his hands. "It was just a word of warning. She'll be fine. Bombshell like that? He'll treat her real nice."

Fuck, Liam was going to be sick. "Then we have a deal?" he ground out.

"Sure, man, sure." Marco typed the information he'd already gotten from Ryu into his phone and pressed a button. He flipped the phone around to show the transfer in progress. Seconds later, Liam's phone pinged a notification that it had gone through.

I don't want to do this.

He didn't have a choice.

She trusted him to hold up his end of the bargain, and he had to do it.

He nodded at Marco. "Pleasure doing business with you." He looked across the lounge and found Kenzie watching him. An almost imperceptible nod and he turned on his heel and walked out the front door.

She could take care of herself. He knew that.

She shouldn't have to.

Liam walked around the corner and down the block to the back entrance to the building. He pulled his coat up around his ears and dialed the number Kenzie programmed into his phone. Seconds later, a low male voice answered. "Yeah?"

"Transfer went through."

"We saw."

"I'm at the back door now."

A soft click and he was able to push it open and step inside. It was early enough that he could run into someone, so he kept his pace even and his gaze up as if he knew exactly where he was headed.

"Take the stairs up. Tenth floor."

He followed Ryu's directions to an apartment door one floor down from the one where Kenzie would be. "I'd rather be on the same floor."

"You don't have a choice. This is the only vacant one right now." The lock on the door clicked green and Liam pushed inside and shut it softly behind him. A quick glance around the place told him that it was an identical layout to Milo's place the next floor up. A minimalist style left him plenty of room to pace between the fragile-looking furniture.

"She shouldn't be in there," he muttered.

"She can handle herself."

Should he tell Ryu about the way Kenzie cracked today? It felt like tattling, like he thought she wasn't up to it. The truth was that she shouldn't *have* to be up to it. "I know she can handle herself. That's not even a question."

Ryu was quiet for so long, Liam thought he might have hung up. "There are a lot of things going forward that will be uncomfortable for various reasons. Trust that she knows what she's doing. I'll call when it's time to move." He hung, up, leaving Liam alone with his thoughts.

Not the best place to be on a night like this.

He kept seeing Kenzie's face when she climbed into the ring. Too-wide amber eyes. Mouth drawn tight with fear and anger. Body shaking despite her obvious effort to get herself under control. In the short time he'd known her, she'd never hesitated, never shown an inkling of fear even when the average person would have.

Then again, the average person didn't spend years being hurt as a child and then have to willingly put themselves in their abuser's control again.

It was only for an hour. She should be able to accomplish what she needed to in that time so he could come in and deal with the rest.

An hour too long from where he stood.

Liam opened the sliding glass door and stepped out onto the balcony. The chilly temperatures of the day had descended into downright frigid with the night. He tilted his head back, looking at the floor of the balcony overhead. Too far to climb, but he still felt closer to Kenzie here. He checked to ensure his phone still got plenty of service and inhaled slowly.

Waiting was always the hardest part.

His phone buzzed and for one heart-stopping second, he thought Ryu was calling with an SOS for Kenzie. Then Liam process the name on his screen. Not Ryu. Aiden.

He sighed. He'd been avoiding his friend's calls for days. Might as well allow himself this distraction and answer now. He moved back into the apartment and answered. "Hey."

"Hey," Aiden said slowly. "That's all you've got? You said you'd be gone ten days, Liam. It's been nearly a month."

Guilt flared, but he tamped it down. "I haven't had a vacation in seventeen years. I'm due."

"No one is questioning whether you're due a vacation. But you fly off with my sister and the Russian and, next thing I know, they're back in New York and no one can reach you."

Now Aiden was just being dramatic. Liam bit back a sigh. "You did reach me. I told you myself over the phone I needed longer."

"That was two weeks ago."

He glanced out the sliding glass door, but nothing appeared to save him from this conversation. "Did something happen while I was gone? Something where you needed me specifically and I wasn't there?" It wasn't fair to put all his frustration on his friend. He knew that. He still couldn't stop.

"You're always there when I need you." The quiet reply took his legs out from beneath him.

Liam slumped onto one of the weird-ass chairs with no backs and sighed. "I found her, Aiden. I just need a little more time."

"Is she coming back to Boston with you?"

He gave himself five full seconds to picture the hell Kenzie would unleash in Boston if she paired up with various members of the O'Malleys. Carrigan or Keira or Charlie. They'd start a fucking riot. His smiled died with the knowledge that it would never happen. "No."

Aiden hesitated. "So what happens now?"

"I don't know. I don't have the answers I need yet."

Another hesitation, longer this time. "Come home, Liam."

"Is that an order?"

Aiden cursed. "No, it's not a fucking order. In all the time I've known you, you've never asked me for shit. You took a bullet for my wife. You've done more than that for the family. Don't you think I know how much we owe you? More than that, you're my fucking friend and I'm worried about you. You've been chasing this specter for years. There's no way for this to end that doesn't rip someone's heart out of their chest."

Liam knew that better than anyone.

He still wouldn't walk away from Kenzie.

He wasn't capable of it. Not anymore.

"I have to see this through," he said quietly.

Aiden sighed. "How much time do you need?"

"I don't know. More." His phone buzzed with an incoming call and Liam cursed. "I have to go. We'll talk later."

"Liam—"

He hung up and clicked over. "Yeah?"

"Get up there. Kenzie's in trouble."

* * *

KENZIE WASN'T sure where it all went so wrong. Probably the second she walked through the door. This wasn't a party like Ryu told her. There were no other girls to help distract the men from her.

Kenzie was the only one.

Four men and Milo.

Shit.

The black guy who opened the door, a big man with a ring through his bottom lip and two handguns in a shoulder holster, grinned down at her. "Cheer up, boys. Marco delivered us something special tonight."

When I get out of this, I'm going to shoot Marco's knees out.

The guy looked at her like she was already naked. "Damn, he's really upped his game, hasn't he?"

Fear spiraled through her, sinking vicious claws into her stomach and chest. She made a habit of taking on fights she wasn't sure she could win, but the only thing she risked with those was bruises and maybe a broken bone or two. These men would do so much worse.

She smiled brightly, clinging to her clueless mask with everything she had. "Hi, handsome."

He pulled her into the apartment, his big hands roving all over her body. Kenzie made herself relax into it. She had to get Milo alone so Liam could take care of the rest. That meant she couldn't start a goddamn brawl the second she walked through the door. From the number of guns in the place, she'd be riddled with bullets before she took three steps.

Not how she was going out of this world.

Not tonight. Not like this.

The guy kept pawing at her as he guided her deeper into the apartment. The open floor concept had worked well when they spied on the place, but she wished for a few more walls with five sets of hungry eyes roving her body.

And there he was. Her own personal nightmare.

Milo sat back from the rest, a cigar in his big hands. He looked much the same as he had before. His face a little weathered. His dark hair thinning up top. His gut pressing harder against his tacky graphic T-shirt. Somehow, it didn't matter.

Just like that, she was nine years old again and shaking in her skin.

Fuck that. I am not back there. I am in charge.

Except Kenzie didn't feel in charge as the big guy behind her gave her a shove that sent her sprawling across the lap of a thin white guy who had the look of someone with a deep relationship with some kind of drug. From the pock marks marring his skin, probably meth. He slapped her ass and laughed. "Fuck yeah."

She had to get control of the situation. Now.

"Boys, behave." She put a little sultry into her tone as she wiggled off the tweaker's lap and straightened her dress. The leather of the couch stuck to her bare skin as she moved. "Give a girl some time to adjust."

Milo laughed. "You really don't know how this works, do you?"

God, even his voice was the same. Gravelly as if he'd just spent an hour chewing rocks. She twisted her hair around a finger and gave him a long look. "What are you talking about?"

"This isn't about what you want. It's about what we want." He grinned, revealing stained teeth. "My boy Henry wants to fuck you on the coffee table. Then he's going to give the rest of us a turn. And once you've screamed yourself hoarse, you're going to suck my cock like a good little girl."

Like a good little girl.

She'd kill him.

Fuck the plan and fuck playing this out. Kenzie was going to kill him right here and now. She shoved to her feet, but an arm hooked around her waist and towed her back. Kenzie drove her spike heel into the big guy's foot and used his surprise and pain to slip free. She kneed him in the balls and yanked his head down to give his face the same treatment. Something crunched, probably his nose.

Good.

"Jesus!" someone behind her said.

You'll be calling for him again before I'm through with you.

She spun—and pulled up short as something cold and metal pressed against her forehead. In the seconds it took her to dispatch her target, Milo had crossed the distance and pulled his gun.

Shit.

He glared at her. "You just fucked up."

"What's wrong, baby? You don't want to put your dick in my mouth now?"

He pistol-whipped her. Even as she saw the strike coming, he moved too fast for her to dodge. Kenzie barely kept her feet as the force of the blow sent her staggering away from him. Damn it. One of these days, she'd figure out how to keep her mouth shut.

Not today, though.

Milo grabbed her by her hair and hauled her to the coffee table. He pinned her by her throat, gun still entirely too close to her face. "Who the fuck are you?"

She glanced around. The guy whose nose she broke was still on his knees and groaning, one of the men at his side. That left the tweaker and the other black guy in the room, both of who had their guns out now, too. Too close to risk her next move.

The door clicked and everyone went still as if holding their breath. Liam burst in like a fucking tornado. He shot the tweaker and the other black guy without hesitation and then turned to Broken Nose and the other.

Kenzie dug into her cleavage for the drug she'd intended to dose Milo's drink with. Beggars couldn't be choosers. She jabbed him in the throat and, when he gasped, dumped the vial into his mouth and shoved his mouth shut.

He went down like a fallen tree, his eyes rolling back in his head.

The problem was he collapsed on top of her, pinning her in place.

Panic flared, hot and thick in her throat. "Get off me, you son of a bitch."

"I'm here, Kenzie. Give me a second." Liam gripped Milo under his armpits and dragged him off her. He unceremoniously dropped the guy on the floor and yanked Kenzie into his arms. "Are you okay? Did they hurt you?"

"I've fine," she rasped.

Liam touched her throat with tender fingers and then the place on her cheek that throbbed in time with her racing heart. "You are *not* fine." His dark eyes went so cold, it left her breathless. Liam let her go and turned toward Milo.

As much as every part of Kenzie wanted to sit back and let him follow through on the promise of violence, she grabbed his arm. "We need him alive."

"He'll pay for this."

It wasn't a question, but she nodded all the same. "This and more."

He gave her a look like nothing she could do to Milo would ever be enough, but Liam didn't know Amarante like Kenzie did. She'd take his sins out of him one by one, and she'd make him suffer while she did it. Maybe it would even be enough.

She looked at the bodies scattered around the living room. Two shots each. They'd been dead before they hit the floor. "Damn, Liam."

"A necessary skillset."

Under different circumstances, she might poke fun at him a bit, but Kenzie didn't feel much in the way of fun at the moment. Exhaustion and adrenaline played havoc with her body, leaving her shaking and more emotional than she wanted to admit. "The car is in the parking garage?"

"Yeah, I left it there before I came up." He dug a set of keys out of his pocket and pressed them into her hands. "We're almost done."

Her lower lip quivered and she cursed herself for that much weakness. "I'm good."

Instantly, he closed the distance between them and pulled her into his arms, holding her so tightly it was as if he believed he could fuse her broken pieces back together. "I'm sorry I wasn't here sooner."

She clung to him, burying her face in his chest and inhaling the clean scent that she would associate with Liam until the day she died. "It was harder than I expected."

"I know." He gave her one last squeeze and stepped back. Trusting her to stand on her own two feet. "We have to move."

She nodded. "Okay."

He glared at Milo like he wanted to kick the man several times in the face, but finally sighed and bent down to haul his unconscious body up into a fireman's carry. "Let's go."

CHAPTER 14

$\mathcal{L}$iam didn't trust the calm on Kenzie's face. It reminded him ice covering a pond. No telling if it was too thin to hold, not until you put your weight on it and broke through into the drowning deep below. Bad enough that she had to face the fucker currently occupying space in the trunk. Worse that it hadn't gone down like planned.

Until his dying breath, he would never forget the sight of that piece of shit's hand around her throat, his gun pointed at her face.

Liam had never wanted to kill someone as much as he had in that moment. Not an enemy of the O'Malleys. Not the evil bitch who'd shot him. No one. All that history faded away when facing down a future without Kenzie in it.

She'd fought him off herself. Had administered the drug before Liam had a chance to save her. Had held herself mostly together through their harrowing journey down the stairs to the parking garage and this eerie silent trip to the airport. She was so much stronger than anyone he'd ever met.

He loved her.

The truth washed over him, as natural and dangerous as the tide. This wasn't about sex and it wasn't about a connection with no basis in knowledge or reality. He loved this woman, and that love would twist him in a thousand different ways before this was over.

He'd have to choose.

Stay or go.

Island of Ys or Boston.

Kenzie or the O'Malleys.

"Liam?"

He tore his gaze from the street to land on her face. "Yeah?"

Kenzie gave him a faint smile. "Thank you. You were right. If I'd tried have do that alone…"

"You would have figured it out," he said firmly. "You incapacitated him. You were going for his gun next."

She narrowed her eyes. "What?"

"If I hadn't come through that door, you would have gone for his guns and accomplished the same damn thing I did. His weight panicked you for a minute, but if I wasn't there, you wouldn't have felt safe enough to have that reaction. You didn't need me to ride to the rescue. They might have got a few lucky hits in, but you would have come out on top."

If anything, she looked even more suspicious. "You're just trying to make me feel better."

"No. I'm telling you my take on how things would have gone down. Yeah, it's opinion, but the only reason you're doubting yourself right now is because that fucker scared you. There's not a damn thing wrong with that reaction, but I'm not going to sit here and pretend I saved you from something you couldn't have gotten through without me."

She crossed her arms over her chest and then twisted in

her seat to face him fully. "Why am I irritated with you telling me how awesome I am?"

"Beats the fuck out of me."

"Me, too." She laughed softly. "I'm a mess. I'll feel so much better once we're back on the island."

Her casual usage of the collective *we* made Liam's chest hurt in the best of ways. As if they were already a unit and there was nothing to discuss. He knew better. They quickly approached a time where the *only* thing that would get them through it was an actual conversation. Not a bet. Not a fight. Not fucking until neither of them could think straight. Just words and intentions and vulnerability. He honestly had no idea how it would hash out.

Liam reached over and laced his fingers through hers. She tensed for a beat and then relaxed into the casual touch, even going so far as to give his hand a squeeze. Yeah, they needed to talk, and soon. But not yet. They finished the drive to the airport in comfortable silence.

The hanger where they were supposed to meet the others —and the plane—stood empty as Liam pulled to a stop. He glanced at Kenzie, but she was already digging her phone out. She put it on speaker. "Ryu. We're at the airport, but the plane isn't here. Wasn't Luca supposed to have landed a couple hours ago?"

Ryu's hesitation barely gave them enough warning. "There's a problem."

She flinched. "I'm going to need you to be less dire and more forthcoming with pertinent details. Immediately."

"Arthur got the drop on Luca and Cami." Another beat. "Luca was shot twice, and it's not good. The plane is still coming, but they had to detour to Thalania to get him patched up enough to make it home."

Her hand shook so badly, Liam had to take the phone for

fear that she'd drop it. He clasped her hand with his free one. "Why not stay there until he's recovered?"

It was Kenzie who answered. "None of us really trust the doctors outside the island. They're our people. Everyone else is suspect."

He wanted to argue that if Luca's life was on the line, surely his woman's countrymen were above reproach, but Liam knew how this worked. The O'Malleys had their doctor, and while they might go to an actual hospital if pushed, it was never the preferable option. "We'll stay put until they get here."

"Everything went well?"

Liam and Kenzie exchanged a look. She gave a patently false grin. "Yep. All peachy and shit. Milo is in our trunk as we speak."

"Good. Things are...complicated here. Get back as soon as you can." With that worrisome statement, he hung up.

Kenzie slumped in her seat and closed her eyes. "That idiot should have stayed in Thalania."

He took a few moments to chew on that, to read between the lines to things unsaid. "His home and family are on the island. I don't think he ever considered it a choice."

"Yeah, well, he should have. We chase down vengeance because we're too fucked up to do anything differently. If we can't have whatever normal happiness looks like, we sure as hell should make sure that no one else ends up like us. But Luca? He has his chance at happily ever after. He fell in love with a *princess*, for fuck's sake. That's a romance yanked directly from fairy tales, right there."

"Most fairy tales are horror stories."

She gave him a long look and then huffed out a breath. "Okay, fine, I concede that point. But *my* point still stands. He has a chance at normal and instead, he's bouncing around the world, dragging his lady love with him and getting shot." Her voice cracked on the last word.

Liam climbed out of the car and rounded the front to pull open Kenzie's door. He took her hand and tugged her out and into his arms. "He's okay."

Her breath shuddered out in a sound that was almost a sob. "You don't know that."

"I know that." He hugged her tighter. "Cami loves him, right? She wouldn't let him get on a plane away from a doctor she trusts if he was anything less than stable. He's not in a position to argue with her, and Cami is more formidable than anyone suspects when they first see her." He could still feel the shock register when the princess looked at him with those big blue eyes and then punched him in the throat without ever losing the sympathetic look on her face. If she thought for a second that it was necessary, she'd tie Luca to a bed and keep him there until it was safe to travel.

He'd do the same for Kenzie.

He held her close as she shook, murmuring soothing nonsensical things, but his mind took a turn for the dark. If Luca was injured badly enough to need immediate transport out, he wouldn't have secured their third target.

They'd send Kenzie after him. Liam had no doubts about that. They needed that man and the knowledge he carried, and they wouldn't take into account that Kenzie was teetering on the edge after the earlier attack. How could they when she wouldn't tell them?

Liam smoothed a hand down her long blond hair. "It will be okay." He couldn't do much that Kenzie wasn't capable of pulling off herself, but he could alleviate this burden for her. She would be distracted with worry about her brother, and Liam would do what it took to ensure she didn't throw herself into danger the first chance she got.

He understood that this was important. The O'Malleys did their part to support the other families in Boston who worked to cut down on the flesh trade, but that was one city in one country in the world. He highly suspected that the enemy the Horsemen sought was responsible for a much larger chunk. If Liam could assist in any way, he'd do it. Both for Kenzie and for the greater good.

He wasn't much of a white hat. Never had been, never would be. But anyone who fucked with kids deserved to be put down in such a way that it made an example of them, that it struck fear into others like them.

The Horsemen were the only ones capable of pulling that off.

* * *

KENZIE DIDN'T DRAW a full breath until she climbed the stairs and walked onto the plane. When she saw Luca, laid out on a gurney that was strapped to the floor. He was too pale, and his chest was covered in bandages. "You fucking *asshole*."

He blinked through the bruises on his face. "Hey, Kenzie."

"Hey, Kenzie," she hissed. "That's all you have to say? I ought to smother you for being stupid enough to get shot *twice*." Luca could have died. She knew that after Ryu's call, but somehow seeing it was so much worse.

Her brother could have *died*.

He blinked at her and then glared. "You're one to talk. Look at your fucking throat. Look at your goddamn face. You let that piece of shit get close enough to choke you *and* hit you. What the hell, Kenzie."

"*Children.*" Cami walked up from the front of the plane, her voice snapping with impatience and fury. She wore jeans and a T-shirt and there were scrapes on her knuckles as if

154

she'd done a number on someone. Her expression dared them to step out of line. "You both made bad decisions and you both are worried about each other. Stop snapping like toddlers and sit down so we can go home."

Kenzie propped her hands on her hips. "Who died and made you den mother?"

"Kenzie, you might be able take me in a fair fight, but in your current state, I would put you on your ass. Sit. Down."

Damn.

Princess really did have some teeth, didn't she?

She sank into a seat as Liam walked through the door with Milo over his shoulder. Cami jerked her thumb over her shoulder. "Put him back there. We have zip ties and a box to keep him in."

"Got it." He disappeared through the door and Kenzie heard him drop the man with a loud thump. Obviously, Liam was holding in some pent-up anger at how things had gone down in the apartment. Not that she blamed him. She was harboring a whole lot in the way of feelings about it, too.

Cami propped her hands on her hips. "I'm going to go supervise. If I hear you two arguing again, I swear to god, I'll tranq you both." She stalked into the room and shut the door most of the way.

Kenzie pressed her lips together, but she couldn't resist poking at her brother. "She's really got a hard-on for that tranq gun, doesn't she?"

"She'll do it, too. She doesn't bluff." He laughed, though the sound cut off with a pained grunt. "Don't get shot. It hurts like a bitch."

"Ditto for being choked out in a seriously non-sexy way." She leaned forward and eyed his bandages. "Ryu has a shitty bedside manner. He dropped the bomb about you being shot and didn't give any details."

"We had everything set up to perfection, but he went after Cami and I lost my cool. My shoulder is still all fucked up from the Wild Hunt and Arthur took advantage of it." He looked out the window. "He got away."

"It won't matter in the long run." After they got back to the island and bandaged up, they'd send Kenzie after him. She actually relished the challenge, the chance to redeem herself. None of her nightmares were linked with Arthur. She'd be able to go through with the extraction without all the emotional turmoil and needing to lean so heavily on Liam.

Not that Liam seemed to mind acting the part of her rock. He simply offered what she needed. No questions asked. He didn't need her to trot out her pain for him to understand that she had shit to work through. It was...nice. Really nice.

Better than nice.

Kenzie's bedside manner rivaled Ryu's for shittiness, but she couldn't let Luca sit there and look so miserable. "It's okay."

"It's not okay." He shook his head. "I'm losing my edge, Kenzie. I can't be trusted for this shit anymore, not when I forget everything the second Cami is in danger."

"She can take care of herself."

"You think I don't know that? No shit she can take care of herself. It's not about that. It's the fact that I love her, and I can't stand the thought of the monsters of our world laying their filthy hands on her. She deserves to be cherished and kept safe, and here I am dragging her into danger every chance I get."

He loved his woman, but hell if he didn't get blinders on when it came to her. Kenzie hesitated, but in the end she'd never been that good at keeping her mouth shut. "If you try to bench her, she'll kick your ass."

"I know that." He sounded so put out about it, she almost felt sorry for him. Almost. But Luca had found love, of all things. True love, the kind that threaded through the pages of all her favorite books.

The kind part of her was convinced she'd never experience for herself.

Fuck that.

Fuck.

That.

Milo and the others took so much from her. They closed pathways to things she hadn't been old enough to know she wanted. She'd be damned before they took this, too.

Kenzie wasn't capable of what passed as a normal relationship, but neither was Luca and he'd still found someone who *fit*.

Liam fits.

She didn't have the strength to push the thought away this time. Maybe before this trip, she could convince herself that everything with Liam was sex and sex alone, but that argument didn't hold water anymore. Not after the last couple days.

"I thought it was a mistake to bring him."

She glanced at Luca. "What?"

"The mobster. I thought it was a mistake. All of it. Amarante should have kicked him off the island the second the Hunt wrapped up. And then I come back and find out you're playing fast and loose with him and…" Luca let out a pained breath. "It's possible I was wrong."

"What?" She gave a mocking gasp. "The amazing Luca was *wrong*. I'd be surprised, but you're on quite a streak when it comes to that lately."

"Tell me about it." He closed his eyes, his voice dropping until she could barely hear him. "I didn't think people like us had a chance to be happy, but Cami proved me wrong. Maybe Liam will prove you wrong."

She sat there trying to come up with a suitable reply for so long, whatever the doctors had dosed him with took hold and swept him under. It was just as well. Kenzie didn't have a good response. She wasn't about to tell her overprotective brother that she was tipping over the edge of no return with Liam.

Had already tipped over the edge.

Was in a total freefall.

Didn't know if she'd fly or break both bones and heart when she crash-landed.

Cami and Liam walked back into the main part of the plane and from the uncomfortable looks on their faces, they'd obviously been stalling in order for Kenzie and Luca to have a conversation. Cami immediately went to him and pressed her hand to his forehead. "Good. He needs rest. I'll tell the pilot that we're ready to get out of here." She moved past Kenzie and disappeared through the door at the front of the plane.

Liam gave her a long look and finally moved to sit in the chair next to her. "How are you holding up?"

"Is that a trick question?"

"Kenzie."

She sighed. "Everything hurts, and I am so tired, I don't know what to do with myself. And…" She looked up into his dark eyes and almost finished that thought aloud. *And I think I've gone and fallen in love with you.*

"It will be okay."

"That's what people say when they have nothing else of value to offer."

His lips quirked. "I promise that it will be okay." He took her hand, lacing his fingers through hers as if it was the most natural thing in the world.

It *felt* like the most natural thing in the world.

This was the moment when she needed to be strong, to stand on her own two feet. To establish some distance between them so he didn't get any funny ideas about what happened once this all fell out. No matter what Kenzie felt, there were pieces moving beyond her control.

Eventually, Liam would have to leave.

Even if Amarante didn't banish him from the island, he had a life to go back to. A city he loved. A friendship that spanned a lifetime. A job that he'd worked his ass off for years to climb to the top. People didn't give those things up. Not for a little infatuation. Not even for the fuck of a lifetime. Even if he was willing, part of him would always resent Kenzie for the loss of so much of his life. He would eventually hate her for it, but even if he changed his mind later, mob people weren't the kind to forgive and forget.

Once a person burned that bridge, it stayed burned.

Making that choice for a fledgling relationship that had existed for the grand total of a week was the very height of insanity. She couldn't let Liam make that choice. Not for her.

If their time in Chicago had done anything, it displayed just how fucked up Kenzie was. She'd been broken a long time ago, and everything healed wrong. It didn't matter what that little girl could have grown up to be, because she'd had that future taken from her before she'd known enough to mourn its loss.

This was her reality.

Blood and death and revenge.

She was just bent enough to love it, even with its thorns and pain and loneliness. Kenzie and her siblings did things that no other group could accomplish. They *would* see this world rid of unspeakable monsters. Who else could say the same?

It was worth the sacrifice, the pain, the sorrow.

It had to be.

She carefully extracted her hand from Liam's. "I'm, uh, going to try to get some sleep." Even as she closed her eyes, she felt his gaze on her.

It's for your own good, Liam.

Better a little hurt now than a catastrophic hurt later.

CHAPTER 15

*L*iam could feel Kenzie withdrawing from him, but he couldn't do anything to stop it. Not without driving her farther away in the process. Instead, he was forced to sit there and keep his mouth shut through the long flight back to the island. When he originally traveled there, he was under the impression that the only way to get on or off the island was by boat or helicopter, but the Horsemen kept a small runway on the island solely for personal use.

As they touched down, he couldn't stop himself from taking her hand again. "It will be okay."

"I know." She didn't say it like she believed it, though.

Fuck, but he'd give everything he had to be able to see inside that beautiful head of hers. "Kenzie." He waited until she looked at him. "It will be okay."

This time, she managed a small smile. "I know. This was just harder than I thought it was going to be."

That, at least, he could help with. "Why don't you go ahead with your brother and I'll handle Milo?"

Her mouth thinned. "It's fine. You don't have to shield me from him. He's at *our* mercy now."

"Letting me help out doesn't mean you're weak."

"I know that." Her amber eyes flashed, and she seemed to make an effort to get control of her temper. He hated that control and the barrier it built up between them. Finally, she shook her head. "You're right. I'll go with Luca and Cami. Amarante will send someone to help you with him."

He knew better than to comment on the capitulation. "And after?"

"I'll come to your rooms. Just... Just wait for me there."

Shutting him out.

The worst part was he couldn't *do* anything. He couldn't force her to allow him close, to reclaim the intimacy they'd carved out together both on the island and in Chicago. "I'll wait for you." *For as long as it takes.*

She hesitated, and then nodded and followed the rest of them off the plane. Luca took a slow breath and then another. It stood to reason that Kenzie would need space. This trip had rattled her to her core, and anyone would need time to step back and recover from that. He understood, even as he hated the new distance between them.

Several long minutes after the sound of their vehicle had faded into the distance, he rose and walked into the back room where they'd kept Milo for the duration of the flight. Liam hefted the lid off the box to find the man awake. Mile sneered. "You're making the biggest fucking mistake of your life."

"Doubt it." He hauled Milo over his shoulder, ignoring the curses and threats, and walked through the plane and out into the sticky jungle heat. It was almost a relief after the cold of Chicago. This place wasn't home, but there was a comfort in knowing that they'd see any enemies coming from a long way off.

Except Liam wasn't one of them. *He* was an enemy in

some of the Horsemen's eyes. The thought killed what little feel-good he had left.

He shouldn't have been surprised at the woman behind the wheel of the cart that drove up. Death. Amarante. She wore one of her flawless suits and had her long hair pinned back in a way that made it look like a short cut. Large sunglasses hid her dark eyes. "Well done."

"Wasn't me." He hefted Milo into the back and hesitantly climbed into the passenger seat. "Kenzie went back with Luca."

"I know." She put the cart in gear and then they were off. He wasn't sure where he expected them to hold their prisoners, but Liam *hadn't* expected her to drive to a little dock tucked back from Pleasure. When he looked in askance, she gave the barest of smiles. "We don't like filth dirtying up our home. I would think you'd understand."

"I do." The rare times they needed prisoners held for various reasons, it was never in the O'Malley family home. There were other locations better suited for that sort of thing. "I'm just surprised you're allowing me along for the ride."

"You've proven that you can be useful."

"Thank fuck for that," he muttered.

Liam hauled Milo into the small boat waiting and sat silently as Amarante guided them around the southern coast of the island to a smaller third island tucked there. He'd seen it when he flew in the first time, of course, but Liam hadn't thought much of it. There were thousands of islands in this part of the world, and most of them were too small to be worth anything of value. He'd assumed that this island was numbered among them.

He should have known better.

Another small dock and another short walk, this time

leading to a low building tucked back in the tree line. Stepping through the door was like stepping into another world. There was none of the luxury found everywhere on the main island. No, this building with its thick walls and plain features was nothing but a place to commit ill deeds.

It was a large room with a tile floor that gently slanted down to a metal grate in the middle. A quick glance at ceiling found a hook at a height perfect for keeping someone hanging with their arms above their head. A trio of solid wood cabinets were large enough to hold any number of nightmarish tools. On the far side of the room, there were four doors with keypad locks on the outside.

"Put him in the second room."

He followed her orders, walking to the second door and finding it unlocked. He took Milo inside and dropped him on the concrete ground. No bed, nothing in the room but another drain in the center. Obviously, this wasn't a place designed for long term detention.

Prisoners wouldn't live that long.

Liam waited for Amarante to lock the door, pointedly looking away when she keyed in the six-digit code. If she wanted him to know it, she'd tell him. "You're going to send Kenzie after the third guy. The one who got away."

She turned and walked back to the door, clearly expecting him to follow. "We need all three of them. This should have gone off without a hitch, but we'll adapt as necessary. Ryu is currently tracking Arthur's movements, so we'll have a bead on him when she's ready."

He didn't ask why Amarante wasn't the one to go out, didn't rant that Kenzie had already been hurt enough. These people had their own way of doing things, and if Liam had any chance of carving out something with Kenzie, he had to adapt to it.

You're already acting like it's a sure thing.

Like you've made your choice.

Maybe he had.

As if sensing his thoughts, Amarante turned to him. She still hadn't taken off her sunglasses. "This would be where you head back to Boston. The Horsemen appreciate the help you've given, and if you need something in the future—within reason—we'll see what we can do."

He didn't want a fucking favor. To be this close and to lose Kenzie… Yeah, damn it, he'd made his choice. "Send me instead."

"Excuse me?"

"Kenzie could take this guy, sure, but she's hurt and off her game because of how things went down in Chicago. She needs someone to watch her back. Or, better yet, keep her here and get started on those two fuckers while I handle Arthur."

Amarante stared at him for a long time, her expression unreadable. "Do you care about her that much?"

I love her.

Not words he'd speak aloud for the first time to Amarante. They were reserved for Kenzie and Kenzie alone. "Yes."

"This won't work out how you want it to. She won't thank you for stepping in on her behalf. Kenzie is more than capable of pulling her own weight."

"I know that." All of it. But if the choice was between Kenzie being pissed and Kenzie being safe, he knew which option he would go with every time. "But just because she can, doesn't mean she should have to."

Another of those long looks that told him absolutely nothing. Finally, she sighed and slipped off her sunglasses.

It was everything he could do not to react. Amarante had dark circles beneath her eyes that spoke of endless nights—as if she hadn't slept a single moment since they left. She let him look his fill and then replaces her glasses. "If you're willing to pay the price, then I'm willing to send you." Her lips curled into a smile that wasn't the least bit happy. "We'll both get Kenzie's wrath before the end of this."

He didn't doubt it. "When do I leave?"

"I'll have the plane and information in place in the morning."

One last night to say goodbye, to ground them as firmly as possible before he did something that might break the trust between them for good. It was worth the potential price. It had to be. He couldn't keep Kenzie from rushing into danger time and time again over the course of her life, but he could damn well make sure she didn't take off after a man who'd almost killed her brother while nursing a black eye and still reeling from facing down one of her own personal demons.

Hopefully, she'd forgive him.

Eventually.

* * *

SOMEHOW, Kenzie hadn't realized exactly how hurt Luca was until the small team of the doctors who lived on the island appeared to whisk him away to surgery. *Then* it all sank in with a suddenness that left her reeling. "He's going to be okay." She wanted to say the words with calm confidence. They came out as a question instead.

"If he doesn't..." Cami stood next to her, her arms wrapped around her thin frame. The woman never looked particularly small despite her short height and petite stature, and she had the phenomenal ability to look down her nose at anyone, no matter how much taller than her they were. She didn't look calm or in control right now.

She looked freaked the fuck out.

Get it together, Kenzie.

This wasn't just about her, no matter that she'd known Luca longer, that he was her brother. Cami and Luca were destined for forever, and that meant Cami was an honorary sister.

The Horsemen took care of their family.

She shored up her spine and turned to Cami. "You look like you could use a drink."

"I'm not…" She closed her big blue eyes and took a shuddering breath. "They did the best they could to stabilize him before we left Thalania, but I knew he didn't trust anyone there enough to go under to get the last bullet out. If I had forced the issue—"

"You were right not to." She grabbed Cami's hand. "Have you slept at all since he was shot?"

Cami shook her head. "No. Every time I closed my eyes, I couldn't shake the feeling that I'm going to lose him as soon as I found him."

Fuck.

This was what love did to a person. It brought them to soaring heights and the deepest circle of hell, all in the same week. "He will be okay," Kenzie said, and this time she managed to sound like she knew what she was talking about. "The doctor will come get us when it's done, but we aren't going to do any good standing here and trying to will him to walk through the doors."

"You're right. I know you're right." Cami gave herself a shake. "Okay, yes, I would like a drink."

Kenzie glanced around, but Liam was nowhere to be found. It would take time for him to help transport Milo to the third island and get back. She couldn't stand around here and wait for him, not when Cami needed her support.

No matter how much she wanted to.

She kept her hold on the other woman's hand and led her

167

to one of the doors cleverly tucked away behind a painting. "Come on. Neither of us are fit for the public right now." Cami didn't say a word as she led her through the warren of passages to the hub.

For once, Ryu wasn't glued to his computer or the wall of monitors. He had a bottle of bourbon already opened and three glasses ready. At her raised eyebrow, he said, "We'll wait together."

Luca would be fine. He was well enough on the plane to give Kenzie shit. That had to mean something. Sure, drugs were magical things, but he had to be okay. He *had to.*

They took seats around the small table tucked into the corner of the room, and Ryu poured a healthy amount of bourbon into each of the glasses. They all took long swigs, and Kenzie closed her eyes as the alcohol burned its path to her stomach. When she opened them again, she found Cami and Ryu both lost in their own thoughts. Morose. So fucking morose. If left to their own devices, they'd just sit here in silence and worry until they drove themselves crazy.

Kind of like she was doing in that moment, too.

She stood and went to rifle through Ryu's desk until she came up with an old deck of cards. "How something to keep us distracted?"

"Sounds good," Cami said, her normally sweet voice gone hoarse with worry.

Kenzie raised her eyebrows at Ryu. "Care to test your skills, brother? You're getting rusty in your old age."

"I'm better at cards than you are."

"Prove it."

He snorted. "Deal me in."

Kenzie shuffled a few times. "Luca's terrible at cards. Really, truly terrible. Did he ever tell you that?"

"No." Cami watched her shuffle and took another long drink of her bourbon. "He never mentioned it."

"Probably because he knows if you play, you'll take him for everything he's got." She kept her tone light. "I've never seen anyone so awful at poker. Blackjack should be easy, but he flops every single time. He's even hopeless at Go Fish."

A small smile pulled at the edges of Cami's lips. "Surely it's not as bad as all that."

"It is." Ryu tapped the table. "He can't even hustle card games with a stacked deck."

Cami laughed softly. "I'll be sure to challenge him to a game of strip poker when he's better." A cloud passed her face. "I mean, if—"

"*When*," Kenzie said firmly. "And you better challenge him to something more interesting than strip poker. If he loses enough, he might stop playing with you the same way he did with us." She dealt out the cards with a flourish. "How about some Gin Rummy?"

"Sounds good."

Ryu picked up his cards, a small line appearing between his brows. He treated everything as both life and death hung in the balance. Even a silly card game. Sometimes that frustrated the hell out of Kenzie, but she appreciated the focus in this moment. "Amarante's not back yet?"

"No."

Alarm flashed through her and she almost dropped her cards. "She isn't going to…"

Ryu finally dragged his gaze from the cards in his hand and raised a brow, the expression identical to the one Amarante got when she thought the people around her were acting foolish. She wore it a lot around Kenzie. He picked up a card and discarded. "She's got bigger things on her mind than kicking your lover off the island. Especially when he's proven useful."

Somehow, that didn't make Kenzie feel any better. But

she trusted Liam to be able to take care of himself so she could take care of Cami. Even when facing down her sister.

They played for an hour, drinking and sharing little stories about Luca to keep Cami distracted. To keep themselves distracted. So much of their youth was shrouded in bad memories, but after they'd escaped the camp, there were bright points. They'd had each other. They'd fought their way back from the shadows that threatened to swallow them whole. They'd *flourished*.

The door opened and they all went tense, but it was only Amarante and Liam.

Amarante had brought *Liam* back to the hub.

Wow, Kenzie hadn't seen that one coming. Until Cami, the only people who ever came into this space were the Horsemen. They didn't even allow staff back here to clean, which was something Kenzie bemoaned when she had to scrub her own damn toilet, but the privacy was worth a little bit of work now and then.

Her sister slipped off a pair of sunglasses and walked over to grab a chair, and took a seat between Ryu and Kenzie. "Deal me in."

Kenzie whistled. "You look like shit." Amarante might not travel off the island often, but that didn't stop her from worrying when either Kenzie or Luca did. She always looked like this when they came back—exhausted, as if she spent the entire time pacing and waiting for news.

Amarante raised a single eyebrow. "You're one to talk."

Since Liam was still lingering in the doorway, Kenzie made the decision for him. She got up, grabbed one of Ryu's computer chairs, and dragged it over to the spot on the other side of her. "Sit. You're making me nervous with all the lurking." The table wasn't meant to hold more than four, but she wasn't about to let that stop her.

"I'm not lurking." He sank down next to her and reached

under the table to squeeze her knee. Just that, but it was enough to uncoil something tight and unhappy in her chest. He was okay. They were okay.

Now Luca just needed to be okay.

Another hour passed and Ryu beat them all soundly at round after round of Rummy. When the phone finally rang, it was Amarante who jumped up and strode to answer. "Yes?" She turned away from them. "Yes, thank you." She hung up and looked over her shoulder. "He came out of surgery just fine. He'll make a full recovery."

Kenzie hissed out a breath and reached across the table to take Cami's hands. "What did I tell you?"

"I didn't doubt you for a minute." But her blue eyes shone with unshed tears. She looked at Amarante. "When can I see him?"

"I'll take you there now."

As much as Kenzie wanted to see her brother, she recognized that Cami needed time with him—time alone to break down without the rest of them hovering over her shoulder. She might trust and love Luca, but the other three Horsemen hadn't earned either from her. Smart girl.

Though they would all fight to the death for her now by virtue of her relationship with Luca, they hadn't exactly made it easy on her during the Wild Hunt.

Once the two women disappeared, Ryu shot back the rest of his bourbon and pushed to his feet. "I'll get back on Arthur's trail."

Because they needed to secure him sooner, rather than later. She finished her drink and stood, feeling a little off-center. "Thanks."

Liam still hadn't said anything. Not while they played cards. Not as Kenzie took his hand and led him through the hub to her private rooms. It wasn't until she shut the door that she realized she'd never brought anyone back here that wasn't family.

As if she needed further confirmation that Liam had worked his way beneath her skin and into her heart. "Shower?"

"Yeah." He followed her into the bathroom. It seemed the most natural thing in the world to get the double shower heads going and strip. Liam took a few seconds to check her neck and face. "That's going to sting."

"I've had worse."

Something strange and dark flickered through his expression. "I know." He pulled her into the shower.

She hadn't realized how tired she was until the hot water hit her skin, beating away the tension keeping her on her feet. Kenzie swayed. "I think the bourbon went to my head."

"More like a whole lot of adrenaline letdown and no sleep, combined with the bourbon, went to your head." He washed her in the same gentle economic way he had back in Chicago. Caring, but also not the least bit sexual. If she had the energy, she might have been insulted. But she didn't, and so she stood there passively while he gave himself the same treatment.

Kenzie licked her lips, something thick and unwelcome in her chest. "Liam?"

"Yeah?"

"Will you sleep with me tonight? Just…sleep with me."

He smiled slowly. "Yeah, Kenzie. I'll just sleep with you tonight."

Fifteen minutes later, he tucked them both beneath the voluptuous comforter that she'd spent a truly ridiculous amount of money on. Liam let her get comfortable on her side and then he curled his bigger body around hers, a solid wall of warmth and muscle to hold her up and ground her at the same time. He pressed a soft kiss to the back of her neck. "I'm glad your brother is good."

"Me, too." She shuddered. "I... There was a minute there where I thought everything wouldn't be okay. That we could lose him."

"I know. I'm sorry." He held her tighter as she shook. "He's okay. He'll make a full recovery."

"I know," she whispered. "I'm good. I swear." It was like her body had all this pent up feeling and now that the crisis had passed, it was determined to shake it out of her all at once. She turned and wrapped herself around Liam, burying her face in his chest. "Don't get shot, okay? I couldn't stand it."

He smoothed her hair and down her back. "Having been shot before, I have no desire to repeat the process."

"I want to kill that bitch."

"She's been dead for years."

Kenzie clutched him tighter. "Maybe I'll dig her up and shoot her a few times. Just to make sure."

His laugh rumbled through his chest. "Desecrating graves is usually frowned upon." The amusement died in his voice. "I feel the same way, Kenzie. I would do anything to make sure no one ever lays hands on you again. No matter the cost." He tilted her chin up and frowned. "Don't cry."

"I'm not." She blinked rapidly. "I'm having an allergic reaction. Or maybe there's something in my eye. A really big stick."

This time, he didn't laugh. Liam swiped his thumb across her cheeks, wiping away her tears. "I love you."

She went stock still. "What?"

"I love you."

She had to clamp her lips together to keep from questioning him again. He'd definitely said those three little words. The ones she never thought to hear outside of her family, and certainly not with such conviction.

Liam loved her.

"I love you, too," she blurted. "It's really inconvenient and I don't think I like it, but I do."

"Do you trust me?"

Alarm bells pealed through her head. Yes, love and trust were supposed to go hand in hand, and yes, she had leaned on Liam more than a few times over the last couple of days. But his question felt weighted and heavy with meaning that extended far into the future. "Yes," she whispered, praying she wasn't damning them both.

There was still the matter of his entire life being on hold while he stayed on the island. She cleared her throat. "I can't ask you to choose between me and them, Liam. I won't. And my future is wrapped up in the island. How could this possibly work?"

"We'll figure it out."

She gave a hiccupping laugh. "That's what someone says when they don't have a plan and have no idea how they're going to figure it out."

"Trust me, Kenzie." He kissed her forehead, each of her cheeks, her lips. "Trust that we'll get through this together."

She didn't have it in her to figure out the fine details tonight. Tomorrow would have to be good enough for that. They could do it together.

Together.

A word that could mean so little, but also could tip her whole world on its axis. Before Liam, *together* always meant her and her siblings. A united front. Them versus the rest of the world. They took care of each other, they kept each other safe, but there were some needs that simply couldn't be met in that kind of relationship.

Liam's declaration promised to at least try.

Together.

"Okay. Together."

He gathered her close again, the steady beat of his heart lulling her into something resembling peace. Tonight, things were okay. Better than okay. They had accomplished the goal of bringing Milo in. Luca would survive to fight another day. Liam was here in her bed, telling her that the loved her. Spilling words to back up the truth he demonstrated time and time again with his actions.

It was almost—almost—enough to let her relax.

There were other battles to fight, though. Tomorrow, they'd have to form a plan to go after Arthur again, and this time they wouldn't have surprise on their side. She didn't relish a repeat of Chicago, but Kenzie was sure she wouldn't freeze up the same way she had when facing down a specter from her past.

Doubt threatened to creep in, though. She'd never faltered before. Not really. What was to say that it wouldn't happen again? Every opponent Kenzie had dealt with since they founded the Island of Ys was one she knew without a shadow of a doubt she was better than. Yeah, she lost sometimes, but they were small battles in the overall war.

This felt different.

Now she had more to fight for...and more to lose.

If Liam was any less skilled, he might have ended up with a few bullet wounds during that fight in the apartment. He could have *died.* Because Kenzie dropped the ball and didn't hold up her end of things.

She couldn't let it happen. He'd seen enough pain without her adding to the balance. Tomorrow, she'd pull Ryu aside and see about hopping on the plane. Amarante had shown her own kind of approval for Liam in allowing him into the hub, so she wouldn't banish him while Kenzie was gone.

Yeah, that would work.

She'd go after Arthur, extract him, and haul his ass back here for questioning. Liam wouldn't like it, but Liam didn't get a choice in the matter. She wouldn't let anyone else get hurt for this vendetta.

After all, it was better to ask for forgiveness than permission.

CHAPTER 16

*K*enzie woke up alone. Her body registered that truth before her mind did. Even then, she tried to deny it. She touched the spot on her bed where Liam had slept last night. It was cold.

Damn it.

She sat up and shoved her hair out of her eyes. Any hope that Liam had just wandered away to take the world's longest shower dissipated as she looked around her room and realized both his clothes and bag were gone.

Kenzie climbed out of bed and yanked on the first thing she laid hands on—an oversized T-shirt that she'd stolen from Ryu so many years ago that he'd *finally* stopped asking for it back. She stalked into the hub, fury bubbling up with each step.

Ryu sat in his usual spot behind his computers and barely glanced up as she slammed her hands onto his desk. "Morning, Kenzie."

"Don't you 'morning, Kenzie' me. Where is he?"

"Who?"

She slammed her hands down again, and then a third time for good measure. "You know who. Where is Liam?"

For the first time in as long as she could remember, Ryu wouldn't quite meet her gaze. "You should talk to Amarante."

Cold slithered down her spine. "If she did something to him…"

"Not that." Ryu shook his head. "Give us a little credit."

"I'm giving you exactly as much credit as I'd give myself in your situation." If she thought someone was taking advantage of Ryu, she'd bury the bitch. Granted, that would require her reclusive brother to actually leave the hub and interact with people, but the point stood. "Where. Is. He?"

"Not on the island."

Kenzie pushed off the desk and stared. No. He wouldn't. But the implacable expression on her brother's face confirmed her suspicion. "Where is Amarante?" she bit out.

"Luca's room. He's doing well, and Cami needed to sleep, but she didn't want him to be alone."

She didn't bother to reply as she turned and stalked away. They maintained a regular staff of doctors and nurses on the island, and kept them tucked near the hub in the center of Pleasure. Though the rooms had access to a public hallway, Luca was in the one reserved for Horsemen use only. It wasn't utilized often, but occasionally one of their staff would need to be bandaged up, and there was the Great Flu Scare of 2016 that had seen a shit ton of people come through the doors.

Luca was sleeping in his bed, and his color already looked better than it had the day before. Kenzie walked to his side and looked down at him, measuring his breathing against her own. He would be okay. She knew that, rationally, but seeing him in a hospital bed was twelve different kinds of wrong.

No use ignoring the reason she'd come here, though.

She turned to face Amarante. Her sister sat in a chair on

the other side of the bed, a laptop balanced on her lap. Amarante kept typing. "You have something to say."

"Where is Liam?"

"Why ask me?"

Kenzie hated that they had to go through this song and dance, hated that Amarante was playing games again and wouldn't just tell her what the fuck was going on. She propped her hand on her hip and glared at her sister. "Because, Te, you are queen of the motherfucking island, and nothing goes on here that you don't know about. I know you'd cut off your hand before you let someone like Liam wander off, so I know *you* damn well know exactly where he is."

"Queen of the motherfucking island," Amarante mused. She finally set her laptop to the side and gave Kenzie her full attention.

"That's what I said.

She narrowed her eyes. "Don't stop there. Tell me how you really feel."

Great. They were going to do the Amarante Ice Queen to Kenzie's Drama Freakout. Amarante was only four years older than her, and yes, she had taken on an almost parental role at first, but that didn't excuse that patronizing bullshit right now. Kenzie spoke through clenched teeth. "You are our leader, and I have never made qualms about that. No one has. So don't get your panties in a bunch just because someone is finally stating it out loud. You say jump, and we are more than happy to jump. *We* agreed to that. Liam did not."

"He's not one of us."

That's what it always came down to. For Amarante, the world fell into two categories: the Horsemen…and everyone else. Liam was firmly among the latter. Kenzie had to look away, because she didn't trust herself in that moment. "I care about him."

"You love him."

Hearing the words spoken aloud shocked her enough to have her rocking back on her heels. "What?" She'd barely allowed herself to admit the depth of her feelings to Liam and here Amarante was, throwing them out there as if it were a fact. As if it had been a fact for a very long time. Kenzie clenched her fists. "Did you send him away because of that?"

Her sister blinked. "Your high opinion of me is noted."

"Don't give me that shit. I know exactly the lengths you would go—and have gone for us. What's wrong with Liam that he's not good enough?"

Amarante pushed to her feet in a rare display of agitation. "First Luca and now you. It's a blow to know how little you think of me. I never would have let the princess die for our plans, and I sure as hell wouldn't repay the mobster's loyalty to you with pain."

That brought her up short, but it didn't dissolve her anger. The fact remained that Liam was gone, and Amarante was the one who sent him away. "Where. Is. He?"

Amarante tucked a strand on her long black hair behind her ear. "You won't believe me, but it was his idea." Something in her expression softened, just for a moment. "He wants to keep you safe."

He wants to keep you safe.

Kenzie's stomach dropped out. "You wouldn't dare. *He* wouldn't dare."

"He flew out several hours ago. He's halfway to Madrid by now."

Halfway to Madrid and without anyone to watch his back. Liam was good, but so was her brother and look what happened to him. The thought of Liam bleeding out in some room, dying alone... Her breath snagged in her chest, stalled by a band tightening around her lungs. Liam could *die* and it would be her fault. The only reason he was doing this was because of her, because he didn't believe she was strong enough to hold her own. Instead of talking to her, he took matters into his own hands and went behind her back to her fucking sister.

If he survived, she was going to kill him herself.

Kenzie smoothed down the fabric of her oversized T-shirt. "I'm taking the helicopter to the airport on the mainland."

"Are you sure?"

"Have I ever failed you, Amarante? Even one single fucking time?"

Her sister looked at her for a long moment and slowly shook her head. "You know you haven't."

"Then you should have given me the benefit of the doubt with this. You should have *talked* to me instead of playing god with both our lives." She turned to the door. "If he dies, I'll never forgive you." Kenzie ignored Amarante's sharp inhale and left the room. She didn't see anyone on her way back to the hub, which was just as well. In her current mood, she couldn't guarantee what she'd do.

Ryu was waiting for her the second she walked through the door. "It's not her fault."

"Amarante does not need you to fight her battles."

"She does when it comes to family." He stepped in her way, forcing her to stop or try to go through him. Ryu cursed. "She's doing what she thinks is best."

"Amarante's always doing what she thinks is best. That doesn't mean it's okay." Kenzie realized she was yelling and made an effort to lower her voice. "He could die, Ryu. Luca would have if Cami wasn't there."

Her brother's jaw worked and he finally sighed. "Then we better go."

"*We.*"

He didn't respond. Just turned and disappeared in the direction of his rooms. Kenzie stared after him for a long moment and then sprang into motion. They had hours of traveling ahead of them, and she'd get her answers then. Right now, the only thing that mattered was making it to the mainland and getting on the next flight out. She had to hope that Liam wouldn't rush into trying to grab Arthur without some planning involved, which meant they had a small window of time to get to him before he did anything too dangerous.

That was assuming, of course, that Arthur wasn't already on the lookout.

The number of things that could go wrong with this situation made her head hurt. It didn't matter. She'd get to him before he was hurt. She would ensure he didn't die for her.

Then, and only then, Kenzie would figure out what she was going to do about the horrible sinking feeling in her chest.

* * *

LIAM HAD SPENT the day watching Arthur. The man was polar opposite from Milo. Apparently the attack from Luca hadn't been enough to keep him holed up, because he moved from business to business as the day progressed, appearing to meet with the owners. From the file Ryu provided, it appeared Arthur was in Madrid to keep up on his boss's business prospects. Keep the people farther down the ladder in line. It should have made Liam's job easier.

He couldn't shake the feeling that it was all a set up.

Not the meetings. Those appeared to be on the up and up.

But the sheer brazenness of the man to walk down the sidewalk as if he hadn't a concern in the world? Yeah, he was daring someone to try something. Maybe he thought he'd killed his attacker. Maybe he just flat out didn't care.

Liam had met men like him before, and they were a different kind of dangerous. One he couldn't afford to underestimate.

Arthur finally went back to the hotel he was staying in at midnight. Liam didn't look up from his phone as the man strode across the lobby. That was one advantage he had—a hotel was a hell of a lot easier to break into than an apartment. There were half a dozen scenarios Liam could play out, depending on the next day or two.

He didn't have long.

There had been no update from the island in the hours since he left, and though part of him was worried about how Kenzie would react, the rest hoped that Amarante had been able to convince her to stay put. If anyone could do it, it was Death.

Arthur had disappeared into the elevator. He was on the top floor, which took a special key to get to. A challenge, but one that Ryu was more than capable of getting around. Liam pocketed his phone and went to rise.

He froze at the feeling of something small and sharp pressing against the spot directly between his shoulder blades. *Knife*, his mind helpfully supplied.

A hand gripped the spot where his shoulder met neck, holding him in place. He knew who it was even before her blond hair swept over the opposite shoulder and Kenzie's low voice whispered in his ear. "I am really, really fucking furious with you right now."

Shit.

He tried to bleed the tension from his limbs, but it didn't work. "You shouldn't be here."

"Wrong answer, dickhead." She poked him a little harder with the knife. "Get your ass out of that chair and take a walk with me."

"You didn't have to pull a knife on me to get me to walk with you."

"How would I know? I didn't think I'd have to chain you to my bed to prevent you from rushing off on the first suicide mission you came across, and yet here we are." She guided Liam to the elevators, her hand with the knife dropping to tuck beneath his suit jacket. His woman was so fucking dramatic, but he didn't have the patience to admire it at that moment. Not when she was *here*, in the last place he wanted her. In danger yet again.

"She wasn't supposed to tell you where I went."

"My sister might scare the shit out of everyone else, but I know her buttons." She didn't speak as she used her free hand to push the number to his floor. Liam didn't know what the hell he was supposed to say. He wasn't sorry for doing this. He would bundle her up and ship her back to the island right this second if he thought it'd work.

Obviously, that ship had sailed.

Kenzie waited until he unlocked his door to shove him inside. Liam caught sight of Ryu sitting at the small dining room table, eating a cheeseburger as he scrolled through something on the laptop. "What the hell?"

"You took the words right out of my mouth. What. The. Hell?" Kenzie threw the knife, imbedding it in the frame of the print several inches from Liam's left ear.

He spun on her, welcoming the fury that rose in the wake of fear and surprise. "Wow, Kenzie. You're really putting together a good argument for how you're capable of handling this job. And you wonder why I left you behind."

She stared at him, her body practically shaking. "You can fuck right off with that noise. This isn't your mission. It's not your job. It has nothing to do with you. You don't get to decide if I'm ready or not, Liam. It's none of your fucking business."

"*You're* my business."

"I was." She stalked to him and got into his face. In her heels, they were almost the same height. "That was before you pulled this bullshit. You underestimated me. You didn't trust me. And you fucking *lied* to me."

"I didn't lie," he couldn't help pointing out. "I never made any promises."

"You never made any promises," she echoed. Just like that, her anger seemed to deflate. She took several steps back, her expression closing down in a way he'd never seen before. Even when Kenzie was furious or frustrated, she was animated to the extreme.

Not any longer.

"Kenzie—"

"I think that's quite enough." She walked to the picture frame and yanked the knife out of it. It disappeared somewhere beneath the leather jacket she wore, and she turned to Ryu. "We extract Arthur tomorrow on his first stop. The plane is ready and waiting. Ryu will drive. I'll play damsel in distress, and you'll take him from behind. I'll deal with the hired muscle."

Just like that. As if it was really that easy.

Who was this woman? Kenzie was fire, not ice. But even though she should be furious—*was* furious by her reaction when she arrived—she gave him no indication of it.

"You made the plan last time and look how that worked out." Even as he spoke, he cursed himself for going there.

Kenzie didn't react. She moved to Ryu and snagged a fry from his plate. "You can do this our way, or I can lock you in that room until it's over. Your choice." As if she didn't care one way or another.

Liam wrestled his frustration under control and made an effort to moderate his tone. "Can we talk? Privately?"

She propped a hand on her hip. "So now you want to talk? Cute."

He'd fucked up. Fucked up by making this call on his own. Fucked up from the moment where he left her bed and got on a plane without her. "Kenzie—"

"Believe me when I say, I really don't give a damn what you're about to say. This week might have been whatever it was, but it's obviously given you the wrong impression about me. I am *War*, Liam. I might miss a step from time to time, but I'm here to fuck shit up and make people pay. It's what I do, and it's what I'm good at." Fury flashed through her amber eyes, hot enough to burn him alive. "You know what I'm *not* good at? Sitting at home like some little mob housewife and wringing my hands while you go off to fight my battles like an idiot."

"That's not—"

But now that the dam had burst, there was no stopping her. "Joke's on me, though, because I thought you actually saw me. I thought that since you were so ready to tell me that you loved me, it actually *meant* something. Instead, you just want to shove me into a box that fits *your* comfort level. That's shitty, Liam. That's so shitty, I don't even have words to tell you how shitty it is." She didn't yell. Every word came out with a painful clarity that spoke of entirely too much time imagining this conversation. "I'm done. If this is what love is, I want no part of it."

The floor dropped out from beneath his feet. "Kenzie, wait."

"No." She held up a hand, stopping him in his tracks. "I'm not going to dim myself so that you can feel comfortable, and *you're* never going to be comfortable unless you can lock me away to protect me. We're at odds, and I'm not willing to compromise. Are you?"

"What's wrong with wanting to protect you? I just fucking found you again, and every time you go on one of these missions, you endanger yourself. Milo would have killed you!"

Kenzie flinched. She actually fucking *flinched*. "He would have killed me." She gave a soft, sad little laugh. "I guess that answers whether you were bullshitting me on the car ride to the airport afterward. You never thought I could take care of myself. You lied to me."

"That's not what I meant." He scrubbed his hands over his face. "You're tangling my words."

"I think I'm interpreting them rather clearly." Kenzie shook her head. "Either help with this extraction or don't. It doesn't matter to me. But when you get on a plane to leave Madrid, you're going back to Boston."

"Wait a damn minute." He took a step forward, and brought himself up short as Ryu rose behind Kenzie. In the few times Liam had interacted with him up to this point, he'd been bland and quiet and almost forgettable, at least compared to his more vivacious siblings. Not now. He looked at Liam as if he wanted to skin him alive, as if he'd done it before and wouldn't blink at a repeat experience. The danger in that single expression was enough to have Liam raising his hands slowly and taking a small step back. "We're going to talk about this later."

"We really aren't."

Kenzie turned and walked into one of the two bedrooms the suite had to offer, Ryu on her heels. The man stopped in the doorway and turned to look at Liam. "You're going to respect her wishes."

He wanted to stride over there and knock the asshole out of the way and continue the conversation, but that was his frustration talking. He'd already learned time and time again that he couldn't steamroll Kenzie into doing shit. If she would just *listen* to him she'd understand what he was trying to accomplish by facing down this extraction without her. But no, Kenzie and reason had never been on the same page.

He cursed and stalked to the other room. She was pissed now, and that was fine. Once this was over, they would talk. He'd explain himself. She would get over her shit and listen. They'd figure out a way forward.

That had to be what happened. This couldn't be over, not over some bullshit like this.

Liam *saw* Kenzie. He knew she was good—better than most people he'd ever come across. Wanting to protect her had nothing to do with thinking she couldn't handle her shit. It was more him believing that she shouldn't have to. Even with her siblings, she'd stood on her own for so fucking long, Liam wanted to relieve some of that burden for her. To give her someone to lean on.

All he got for his trouble was a kick in the nuts.

They'd fight. They were good at fighting. And then they'd figure it out.

He refused to believe that it was actually over. Not after everything they'd been through. Not when the woman he loved was finally within reach.

If it was…

Losing her would break him in a way that nothing else had been able to up to this point.

CHAPTER 17

*K*enzie dropped onto the bed the second Ryu shut the door and pressed her hands to her face. "I am *done* crying over that asshole."

"Kenzie."

"Don't *Kenzie* me. You heard what he said. He lied to me." She'd suspected as much. She simply hadn't thought it'd hurt so much to hear how little he thought of her. Oh, Liam loved her. If she had doubts about everything else, she had no doubts about that. It wasn't enough. Even in her romance novels, love wasn't enough. Relationships took hard work and trust and he'd just torpedoed that right out of the water.

Because Liam didn't trust her.

And he'd proven that she couldn't trust him.

"I hate this." She flopped down onto her back and stared at the tasteful blue of the ceiling. "I hate this so much.

Ryu looked at her for a long moment and then moved to sit next to her on the bed. He laid down next to her, his shoulder barely brushing hers. "Do you want to talk about it?"

No. Yes. She didn't know. What was the point of going

over her feelings on the matter when it was over and done with? She rubbed her chest, as if that touch could smooth away the jagged pain beneath her skin. "I don't know. Do you have some sage wisdom to offer?"

"You're asking me if I have romantic advice for you?"

She made a face. "When you put it like that, it sounds a little ridiculous." Ryu wasn't exactly celibate, but he didn't like being touched in certain ways and that meant he had a very specific criteria when it came to going to bed with someone. They hadn't had any heart-to-hearts about it or anything, but secrets between the four of them were in short supply. "God, we are so messed up."

"We're survivors." She felt his shrug move the mattress. "I'd say we're doing just fine."

That was the problem. Just fine had been...fine. Before. Before she knew how being with Liam would light up a part of her she wasn't sure she'd ever known had existed. At least not outside of theory. She wanted him, in bed and out of it, and even with all the odds stacked against them, she believed they had a chance.

Kenzie should have known better.

Life never hesitated to kick a person just when they thought everything was going to be okay. Why should love be any different?

"I love him," she murmured. "Isn't that fucked up?"

"I don't know." Another shrug. "He's the first one. That means something, doesn't it?"

"It should." She blinked past the burning in her throat, willing it not to reach her eyes. "I don't know what to do."

Ryu shifted onto his side and propped his head on one hand. "What do you want to do?"

"What kind of question is that?"

"The one I asked."

She made a face. "I don't know. I *want* Liam, but when I

look into the future I see constant conflict because he'll always try to shuttle me away from danger and I'll always resent him for not trusting me to hold my own. It's exhausting to even think about."

"Those are the bad times. What about the good times?"

She twisted to face him fully. "What do you mean 'what about the good times?' Those bad times are really bad. He told me that I would have handled it just fine even if he wasn't in that room with Milo. He let me believe that I wasn't nearly as helpless as I felt the moment that fucker wrapped his hands around my throat. And then five minutes ago, he told me that I would have died in that room."

Ryu raised a single brow. "Take out what he thinks. Walk me through what happened."

She didn't want to. She really, really didn't want to. "I misplayed it. I thought I could get him alone, and then I realized too late that private fucking wasn't on the agenda. One of his guys grabbed me and I broke free, but Milo pistol whipped me and got his hands around my throat." She closed her eyes and swallowed hard against the fear the memory brought. Fear like she hadn't felt in nearly a decade. "Liam practically kicked down the door and shot two of the guys. I hit Milo in the throat and shoved those goddamn drugs down his throat. He passed out on top of me and Liam shot the other two."

Her brother studied her for a long moment. "You dispatched Milo on your own."

"Yes?" Where was he going with this?

"Pretend Liam wasn't there."

She huffed out a breath. "But he was there. That's the whole point."

"Pretend Liam wasn't there," he repeated. "Walk me through it."

She closed her eyes, envisioning the room. "He had a

gun." She could almost feel her hand close around it, and Kenzie raised her arm, pointing it first one way and then the other. "I would have shot the tweaker first. Then the guy on the other side of the table. Even with excellent reaction times, I could have handled the other two. Milo played the part of human shield, so they would have hesitated to open fire at me." She motioned as if shooting them. Kenzie opened her eyes. "I would have been fine."

"Yeah."

She sat up. "Why the hell did I get so twisted up about this? Why did he say I would have died?"

"Facing down the people who hurt us isn't easy. You're the first one to be able to match abuse to an actual person. It fucked you up."

She grimaced. "It really fucked me up."

"But you did it," Ryu continued. "Not perfectly, but you handled it."

She rubbed her hands over her face. God, she was so tired. "That doesn't explain why Liam was such a dick about it."

"Kenzie." Ryu chuckled. "He's gone for you. Look at how dumb Luca acted when he was chasing the princess all across the big island. Love makes people act like idiots."

She finally managed a smile at that. "He did act pretty stupid, didn't he?" Realization washed over her. "I'm acting pretty stupid right now, aren't I?"

"Mmhmm."

She grinned. "Look at you! That was some A-plus romantic advice, brother." Kenzie looked at the door. "What am I supposed to do now?"

"There are these neat little things called words. I suggest you use them."

Naturally, everyone became a comedian when Kenzie was off her game. She snagged a pillow and smacked Ryu with it, knocking him onto his back. "I live for the day when you turn into the idiot in love."

"It'll never happen."

She didn't let the certainty in his voice sober her. "Yeah, well, I thought the same thing and look at me now." Kenzie pushed to her feet. She didn't want to talk to Liam. Well, she did and she didn't. It was possible that it would pave the way to a bold new future or some shit.

But it was also possible that it would be the final nail in the coffin of their fledgling relationship.

Ryu sighed. "Don't choose *now* to start being a coward."

"Shut up." She took a breath and charged out the door.

And nearly ran over Liam.

He caught her shoulders, his expression worried. "What's going on? Are you okay?"

What little courage she had left deserted her. Kenzie licked her lips. "Uh… So that conversation you've been dying to have? Maybe we should have it."

He glanced over her head and she didn't know what Ryu did to have Liam tightening his grip on her shoulders, but he towed her across the suite to his room and all but shoved her inside so he could shut the door.

Kenzie glared. "Subtle. Really subtle."

"Your brother is a dick."

"All four of us are dicks. It has nothing to do with gender."

He opened his mouth, seemed to reconsider his next statement, and closed it. "I'm sorry."

"What?"

"I'm sorry," Liam repeated. "I fucked up."

That had been way easier than she expected. Kenzie frowned. "Is this a trick?"

"No." He moved closer and lifted his hand to brush his fingers along her throat. "It's been barely more than forty-eight hours since I saw that asshole try to kill you. Even knowing you would have gotten out of the situation fine... The thought of you being hurt fucks me up. It's going to happen again and again, because this is your life, and I am going to do my damnedest to make my peace with that."

"What if you can't?"

He shook his head. "I will. The alternate of losing a chance with you is too high of a cost."

She closed her eyes and tried to get her thoughts in order. It was hard with him so close, with his thumb stroking up her jaw and along her cheek. "If you ever try to go over my head to my sister again, it's over. Either we're equals or we're nothing."

"Deal," he said softly. "As long as you give me the same courtesy."

Her eyes flew open. "Excuse me?"

"Were you or were you not planning the exact same move?"

To leave before he woke up and take care of the problem herself so he'd be safe? She managed a slight smile. "Guilty as charged."

"I understand that I have to trust you, but you have to trust me, too."

Easy enough to say. More difficult to put into action. She let herself lean into his touch, just a little. "What happens after this, Liam? Even if we figure out the trust shit and manage to balance out things, that doesn't answer any questions about the future. We don't *have* a future."

"Explain."

She took a careful breath. Why was it so much harder to speak these things than it was to rush headlong into a fight? "Your life is in Boston. Your friends. Your family. You can't just leave them all. And I can't leave the island."

"Kenzie." He waited for her to look at him. "*You* are my future."

"You say that now, but you'll resent me for making you choose."

Liam shook his head. Just once. "Aiden doesn't need me anymore. Maybe he never did. He'll respect my choice, because it's the same one he'd make given the same circumstances."

"But—" Surely he couldn't just leave everything for her. Surely she wouldn't let herself ask that of him.

"Kenzie," he said her name like a benediction. "How can you think that I wouldn't find this fight worth stepping onto the battlefield? Because it's yours, yes, but also because of the stakes. I have done a lot of questionable and selfish shit over the years. The O'Malleys aren't bad people, but their endgame is the O'Malleys. This is bigger. This is a fight I can be proud of."

She gave a wobbly smile. "It's a grand vengeance scheme that's going to kill a lot of people."

"It's justice," he corrected. "And it's going to save even more." He pressed a kiss to her forehead, to each cheek, to her lips. "I love you. I want a future with you. We'll fight and we'll fuck and we'll enjoy the hell out of the fact that our life will never be boring. Sometimes I'll fuck up, and I'll do my damnedest to make it up to you." He grinned. "And sometimes you'll fuck up, and I'll think of really inventive punishments that we'll both enjoy entirely too much."

It sounded almost too good to be true. Kenzie ran her hands up his chest to loop around his neck. "I love you, too. I never thought to have *any* kind of relationship with someone, let alone one that would be so uniquely us, but I want it with you, Liam. I want it so much, it leaves me breathless."

* * *

IT WOULD HAVE BEEN NICE, after their declarations, if they

were able to follow through on the promises they made with words by making use of the bed in his room. Or, hell, get the hell out of Madrid and go back to the relative safety of the island.

Instead, Arthur fucked everything up.

Which was why two hours later, Liam found himself crouched in an alley and hoping like hell this story had a happy ending. He didn't want Kenzie in danger yet again, but she had a point about her being the least suspicious of the three of them.

Especially once she'd changed into torn up jeans and a hoodie and pulled her blond hair back from her face. Without obvious make up, she looked younger. Not innocent. Kenzie would never pass as innocent. But she could be twenty-one and in college. The kind of woman that men still looked twice at, but maybe one who didn't realize how pretty she was.

Or that's the line she spun as she got ready, covering the bruise on her cheek with an impressive skill that spoke of practice. According to Kenzie, men loved that shit, to be the ones to tell a beautiful woman that she was beautiful. As if she didn't have access to a mirror every day of her life.

He snorted to think about it now. His woman had strong opinions, and he loved that about her. What he didn't love was crouching here by Arthur's car in the cold and hoping like hell that everything went off without a hitch inside.

The temptation to burst through the door was almost too much to resist.

"She's fine."

Liam glanced at Ryu. The man was systematically slashing the tires of the black sedan. Their own vehicle was parked just around the corner. "I know she's fine."

"Then relax."

Easier said than done.

He heard her before he saw her. Even her voice sounded younger as she spoke breathlessly to Arthur in what sounded like flawless Spanish. Liam had never bothered to learn another language, and he regretted that choice now. It would be useful to know what she was saying. They'd agreed that she'd go into the bar and innocently ask after the car Ryu had just fucked up, playing the part of good Samaritan.

They came around the corner, the small man next to her looking more like an accountant than someone who was capable of almost killing Luca. He spoke furiously to someone over his shoulder, barking commands.

Ryu melted into the shadows next to Liam, allowing him to take lead. The other man might be dangerous in the way all the Horsemen were dangerous, but he definitely wasn't on the same violent level as Kenzie and Luca and Amarante. Or that's what Liam would have assumed if he hadn't seen the look in the other man's eyes after his and Kenzie's fight. He might not be the most overtly dangerous one, but underestimating him was out of the question.

Liam waited until the group of four stopped next to the car. Arthur and two bodyguards. He held his gun easily at his side. They had to do this quick and quiet to avoid bringing any of the others in the bar out here. They were all in the employ of Arthur or the person *he* was employed with, and they would turn this from an extraction into a bloodbath.

Kenzie made an exclamation and bent over as if she dropped something. As if on cue, both bodyguards checked out her ass in those tight jeans. Liam moved, straightening and raising the gun in a single breath. Two seconds later, both guards lay bleeding out on the ground.

Arthur turned, but Kenzie anticipated him. She swept him off his feet and, when he immediately tried to rise, she kicked him in the face hard enough to have his head bouncing off the concrete. He lay still.

"Kenzie," Ryu murmured. "Overkill."

"Luca could have died because of him. He's lucky I didn't crush his fucking throat."

"Later."

Liam moved with them and lifted Arthur up and over his shoulder. "Let's go."

They hurried to the waiting car and piled in. Kenzie took the driver's seat, and Ryu the front. He passed back a pair of zip ties and Liam wasted no time fastening the man's hands and ankles together. He kept an eye on their back windshield, but no one showed up in pursuit. Kenzie drove them nice and slowly to the airport, obeying all traffic laws. None of them spoke, which was just as well.

Once they reached the hanger, Liam was left to play babysitter while Ryu and Kenzie went to speak with the pilot and grab the drugs that would keep their captive under for the duration of the flight.

Arthur coughed his way back to consciousness and blinked at Liam. He looked around, clearly trying to gauge his surroundings, and shot off a query in Spanish.

"English."

The man glared, and spoke in heavily accented English. "Do you know who I am? You are making a mistake. A huge mistake."

Why did they always say that? As if this man was grabbed on accident and they didn't know exactly who he was and who he answered to. Liam sighed, already bored with the conversation. "That remains to be seen."

Arthur looked around, catching sight of Kenzie as she walked out the plane's door and down the steps to the ground. "That bitch is going to wish she never met me."

Liam forced himself not to react. "That bitch kicked your ass once, and she'd be more than happy to do it again if you run your mouth." He leaned close and lowered his voice.

"You shot her brother, and she's got a vengeful streak a mile wide. And that's not even getting into their other siblings." He gave the man a rough pat on his shoulder. "Can't say I'd want to trade places with you. Word has it that Death is quite the connoisseur of pain in exchange for information—and you have information she wants."

"Death…" The man's dusky complexion went almost green. "You mean the Horsemen…" Understanding dawned. "The man I shot was one of them? I didn't know! How could I know? He attempted to harm me and I reacted. I was justified."

"Maybe if you were pleading your case with anyone but them." He nodded at Kenzie. "As it is, I don't like your chances. They aren't in the mood to be forgiving."

Arthur leaned forward, panic practically seeping out of his pores. "Help me. Get me out of here and I'll make you a very rich man. I'll pay anything. Just don't let them take me."

Liam studied him for a long moment. "You more than deserve whatever pain Death delivers leading up to your last breath. And I, for one, look forward to seeing that punishment delivered to its fullest." Liam opened his door and climbed out of the car. He rounded the trunk in time to meet Kenzie at the other door. "I've got him."

Kenzie gave him a look and wrenched the door open. She frowned. "What did you do to him, Liam?"

"We just had a conversation."

She snorted. "A conversation. Sure."

Once they had Arthur dosed and unconscious, they secured him in the back room. It was only then that Liam put into words the plan he'd spent the drive mulling over. "I have to go back to Boston."

Kenzie froze. Fear then anger and finally calm settled over her expressive face. "Okay."

He might have laughed if they weren't still hanging in the

balance. Liam took her hand and pulled her into his arms. "As much as I want to go to the island and simply stay there, there are things I need to handle in Boston before I can."

"Oh." She relaxed against him and sighed. "This is going to be prickly for a while, isn't it?"

"Probably." He gathered her close, trying to soak up this feeling. "If I don't explain to Aiden in person, he's liable to try and come after me, and I'd rather not have the O'Malleys at odds with the Horsemen."

"We'd put them in the ground."

He laughed. "Maybe."

She looked up at him. "How long?"

"At least a couple days. Maybe longer." He paused. "Unless you want me there for what comes next?"

She took a long moment to respond, but Kenzie finally shook her head. "It's better that you're not, I think. Amarante will take care of it, and by the time you're back, we should have names."

"What happens then?"

"I'll tell you when you get back to the island." Kenzie went up onto her toes and pressed a quick kiss to his lips. "Maybe we can arrange another bet. Something sexy and fun to get this thing started out on the right note."

He looked forward to it. "Give me your best shot."

"Oh, don't worry. I will." With one last kiss, she turned and walked to take her seat, leaving Liam to make his own way off the plane. No goodbyes for them, but it was fitting. This wasn't a goodbye. It was an I'll see you soon.

The sooner, the better.

CHAPTER 18

*K*enzie tried not to brood on the flight back to the island, but Liam's absence grated on her. They'd finally figured their shit out and he was *gone*. A small, unsure part of her couldn't help but wonder if his tune would change once he landed back in Boston. It was easy to get swept up in things on the Island of Ys. They made millions off people because of that very fact.

Maybe Liam was just one of the many.

Except he'd managed to get closer to her than anyone else.

"It will work out."

She glanced at Ryu and gave a small smile. "You're doing that thing where you're giving me relationship advice again."

"Worked out last time."

"Mmhmm. There will be no living with you now." She flopped back against the seat and sighed. "What happens if these assholes don't have the answers we're looking for?"

"They will." Ryu shut his computer and set it on the seat next to him. "But if they don't, then we keep looking. We're playing the long game, Kenzie. We always have been."

Yeah, but she didn't want a setback. Bringing in Milo would hopefully put some of her shit to rest, but he wasn't the only one who'd hurt Kenzie in that place. Delving into this felt like fighting a hydra. For every one they chopped down, five more rose in its place. They took down the Bookkeeper, but she was only able to give them three names. What if these three men gave them more names and so forth? It could be *years* before they made it to the top of this thing.

If that wasn't enough to depress her, she didn't know what was.

"We'll get them." Ryu, as always, divined her thoughts. "It might take time, but we'll do it."

"I know." She turned to watch the blue water reach closer as the plane descended. "I'm just feeling maudlin." Ridiculous to miss a man she'd barely known for more than a week. She'd spent her entire life not knowing what it was to have Liam at her side, and she could handle a few days more while he got his shit in order. Especially since that meant he'd be hers, truly hers.

But it didn't matter how ridiculous it was, because she *did* miss him.

"I say I'll be happy when this is over, but I don't know if that's true. Are we even capable of living normal lives?"

"No," Ryu said gently. "The second we entered that place, normal ceased to be an option." He waited for her to look at him to continue. "But normal people can't do what we do. They can't stop the monsters. We can."

She didn't know if it was enough, but it would have to be.

Amarante met them at the runway. "It went well?"

"As well as can be expected."

Ryu hauled Arthur out of the plane and into the waiting cart. Amarante slid her hands into her pockets and studied Kenzie. "You didn't bring him back."

"He had a few things to take care of first." She didn't technically need Amarante's permission to keep Liam on the island. Kenzie owned a quarter of it, after all. But... "I love him."

"Yes."

"He's coming back to the island, and then he's going to stay."

A small smile tugged at the edges of Amarante's lips. "Does this mean you forgive me for allowing him to attempt to nobly sacrifice himself?"

As if it were even in question. Kenzie looked out at the ocean and back at her sister. "We're family. That means we fight and things get fucked up sometimes. You made the wrong call, and nothing you can say will make me think otherwise. That doesn't mean I'm going to hold a grudge for the rest of our lives."

"How kind of you."

She rolled her eyes. "Yep. That's me. Kind." Kenzie hesitated. "If you ever do that again—if you try to make me choose between our family and Liam—you won't like the outcome."

Behind her sunglasses, Amarante's brows rose. "Oh?"

"He's willing to give up everything he's ever known in order to be with me. To join our fight. I can't ask him to do anything I'm not willing to do, and if you try to force the issue or pull some high-handed manipulative shit, then I'll make the same call." It would kill part of her to break with the only family she'd ever known, but she'd never felt for another person what she felt for Liam. That was worth fighting for.

Amarante sighed. "You don't need my permission to choose to be with someone, Kenzie."

"No, I don't," she agreed. "But I want your blessing. I don't want bullshit lingering between us."

"As I told Luca a couple weeks ago, I'm not here to play

the villain in this story." She turned to look at where Ryu stood just out of earshot. "I want you happy. If this man makes you happy, I'm not going to stand in your way any more than I did with Luca and the princess."

"Thank you."

Amarante nodded. She tilted her head one way and then the other, stretching her neck, and rolled her shoulders. "Shall we begin?"

"No time like the present."

* * *

LIAM HADN'T EXPECTED Aiden to meet him at the airport… but he should have. As he walked into the baggage claim, his friend leaned against a wall, looking out of place in the midst of all the rumpled travelers in his expensive suit. It was more than that, though. Even when he toned it down, Aiden had an air of danger about him that people responded to on an animal level. Normal people avoided him, parting around his spot like a river parted around a rock.

Liam stopped in front of him. "You didn't have to come."

"You've been gone nearly a month. Did you really think I'd send someone else to pick you up?"

"I thought I'd call myself a cab."

Aiden shook his head. "You have bags?"

"No." He probably should have bought a bag and some shit to put in it in order not to raise eyebrows for an international flight, but Liam had been too impatient to get back to Boston—and then turn around and leave again.

A subject he had to bring up to Aiden sooner, rather than later.

They walked to the car and drove back to the O'Malley family house in easy conversation. Aiden updated him on the various events that had gone down while he was out of town.

Business was good. There hadn't been any issues of note there. The family, on the other hand, was as batshit crazy as always. Now that most of them had kids of their own, the drama all centered around that kind of insanity. Like Aiden's step-niece having an issue with a friend that brought *all* the family into the argument—both the Irish side and the Russian. Or Aiden having to step in when his middle brother, Teague, got into a conflict with his oldest daughter's teacher.

Batshit. Crazy.

They headed into Aiden's office, and the man wasted no time in pouring them both a strong drink. "No one told me being patriarch of the family meant I'd be dealing with more parent-teacher issues than people trying to fuck with business."

Liam accepted the glass and sank into one of the chairs across from the desk. "It looks good on you. How's Charlie doing?"

"She's still sick as fuck. Whoever called it morning sickness was a lying asshole." He grimaced. "Last week, she threw a plate of spaghetti at my head because the garlic made her nauseous."

Liam laughed. "Sounds like pregnancy is agreeing with her."

"The kid isn't even here yet, and he's already making a bid to be an only child." Instead of sitting behind the desk, Aiden took the other chair. He sat back with a sigh. "You're going back to the island."

He might have laughed if the situation was different. It shouldn't have surprised him that his friend picked up on his intentions even before he had a chance to voice them. Aiden kept the people around him safe by anticipating what people would do in any given situation.

Liam took a long drink. "That thing you have with Charlie? That's what I have with my girl." If Aiden was anyone else, he'd leave it at that, but they had shared too much history. "I love her. I want to be with her, and that means going to the island, because she's not able to come here."

He sat back and looked around the office. How many meetings had they held there over the years, both formal and informal? He couldn't begin to count. He'd miss this place. "It's more than that, though. For a long time, you needed me here to watch your back. Things were in flux, and I could play the part of the constant so you could focus on the important shit."

Aiden frowned. "That's not all you were to me. We're friends."

"We are friends. But we're also not equals. Not in this house." Liam held up a hand to forestall him. "I'm not complaining. Truly. It's not something that bothers me, past or present. My point is that you don't need me anymore. Shit is good here, and the family is stable enough to deal with anything that rises up in the future."

"Your girl's life isn't stable."

Liam smiled. "Not by a long shot. They need another gun in their holster. I have a skillset to be useful in a fight that's going to right a lot of wrongs that have been done to people who don't deserve it."

"I see." Aiden nodded slowly. "I hope you know that you'll always have a place here." He gave a sharp grin. "And if you don't come back to visit regularly, I'll bring the whole clan down there and let them wreak havoc."

Liam allowed himself a full five seconds to picture the various members of the O'Malleys—both this generation and their children—getting underfoot and causing Death no end of trouble. It was a nice thought, even if he doubted Amarante would appreciate the experience. "Once we see this thing through… That might be nice. Even if you meant it as a threat."

He laughed. "Noted." Aiden took a long drink and set his glass aside. "How long are you back for?"

"I have a few things to get in order, but you've operated this long without me, so I expect there shouldn't be much transition involved."

"Your cousin has stepped up admirably."

"Good." He'd have to talk to Mark before he left. They weren't particularly close, but he was one of the few members of Liam's family that he could stand. "Then I'll be here a day or two."

Aiden smiled. "As sorry as I am to see you go, I'm glad you found what you were looking for."

Who he was looking for.

Liam pressed his hand to his chest. He'd left Kenzie in Madrid a little over twenty-four hours ago, but he missed her. This thing between them felt so new, if not untried, and he resented the distance between them. No matter how necessary. "Me, too."

The sooner he got back to her, the better.

* * *

KENZIE WOULDN'T CALL herself squeamish under normal circumstances. Even by a serious stretch of the imagination, torture couldn't be considered normal circumstances. The few times Amarante had needed to delve to those depths, Kenzie didn't stick around to witness it. Bad enough to know what was happening, to see the random fleck of blood that her sister missed during clean up. There was no need for her to sit through the entire thing, not when she was in danger of losing her lunch over too much gore.

A plain old fight? Kenzie could hold her own and then some. Blood and broken bones and the like were just part of the deal. But there was something about having one person chained down and helpless that made her queasy and skittish.

None of the old rules applied this time.

Not with Milo chained to the chair in the middle of the room.

She wouldn't participate, *couldn't* participate, but she still stood as witness.

Ryu had a chair positioned a few feet from her. He always sat in on these sessions, but it was more out of support of Amarante than because he had strong feelings one way or another about torture.

Amarante slowly circled Milo, as if she could tell his weaknesses from a single glance. She finally came to a stop in front of him and bent down. With his wrists and ankles fastened to the chair—and the chair bolted to the floor—he wasn't a danger, but she still stayed out of reach.

"You stupid bitch." He spat. "You don't even know what's going to happen to you because of this. I know people. Really scary people who will take great pleasure in fucking you up."

"I know." From her position, Kenzie caught Amarante's soft smile. Her dark eyes had gone completely empty, as if the part of her that made her *her* had checked out. This wasn't Kenzie's sister anymore. It was Little Death, a name she'd gone by when they first met all those years ago.

Amarante tucked a strand of her long black hair behind her ear. She had removed her tailored jacket and rolled up the sleeves of her mint green button-down. Really, she looked like she was about to sit down for a nice long chat. Even her tone was conversational and easy. "Would you like to know how I know?"

"I don't care, you stupid bitch."

If anything, her smile widened. "I know because I was there."

For the first time, Milo looked less than sure of himself. "What are you talking about?"

"That evil little hell your people created. The one where they sent children" Amarante's tone became even gentler. "Camp Bueller."

The reaction was instantaneous. Milo went rigid and, if he'd been pale before, it was nothing to how all color leeched from his face. It gave him the look of a dead man walking, which was more than a little apt.

"No," he whispered. His gaze jumped to Ryu and then to Kenzie. For the first time, recognition rose, quickly followed by horror. "*No.*"

"All debts come due in time, Milo." Amarante almost sounded like she was apologizing. It made her ten times scarier than if she'd shouted. She turned to her tray of instruments. "I'm about to call in yours."

And then she began.

Kenzie tried to watch, to witness, to even appreciate the payment of his monstrosity coming due. Thirty minutes in he started begging, and it was too much. She moved closer to Ryu, letting his presence and Amarante's back shield her from the worst of it.

And then Milo spit out a garbled name and everything froze.

Ryu shot to his feet. "Repeat that."

"Fai Zhao."

Kenzie looked from Ryu to Amarante and back again. She swallowed her questions about her siblings' reactions through sheer force of will. There would be time for them later, and they needed a unified front.

Amarante didn't turn, didn't seem to breathe. "Please leave, Kenzie."

"But—"

"Now."

209

Her protestation had been half-hearted at best. It wasn't until the door closed, leaving her on the outside and them on the inside that she realized she recognized that name. Where had she heard it before? She headed for the dock, letting her long strides eat up the ground, letting the sun and heat drive away the cold memories of her time in that room.

Maybe it was the walking that dislodged the information. She always had thought better on her feet. Even so, Kenzie nearly tripped over her own feet when the truth hit her.

"Holy fuck, that's Amarante and Ryu's father."

* * *

NEITHER RYU nor Amarante came back to the main island that night. Kenzie paced the hub, trying not to worry, but losing the battle. Luca wouldn't be allowed back in his own rooms for another couple of days at least because the doctors wanted to keep a close eye on him, and Cami barely left his side. As tempting as it was to lay her new knowledge out to him, she knew exactly what he'd do once he found out—he'd yank all his IVs out, jump on the first boat he found, and ride over to the small island to demand answers.

Kenzie couldn't let it happen.

She spun to pace back across the room and skidded to a halt. "How the hell did you get back here?"

Liam gave a small smile. "I have a good memory, and Amarante didn't bother to hide how to open the door from the room we came through last time." His smile fell away, replaced by a concerned from. "Is everything okay?"

"Not even a little bit." She threw herself into his arms, letting his strength push away the worst of her worries. Kenzie wasn't alone. Things might be more complicated than she could have dreamed, but in the end it didn't matter. It *couldn't* matter. They would take down the person responsible, no matter who they were.

No matter how they were related to two of the Horsemen.

When Amarante and Ryu got back, they'd talk and they'd plan and then they'd enact the next steps. It was as simple and as complicated as that.

"Kenzie?"

Some truths were too terrible to hold in, though. She clung to Liam. "The person responsible is... Liam, it's Ryu and Amarante's *dad*." Their own father put them in that place. She could barely wrap her mind around it. She didn't want to.

"Fuck," he breathed. She felt him turn to look at the doorway he'd just walked through. "Where are they?"

"Still, ah, interviewing our guests." They would confirm the information. No one would act before they knew the truth. Even if the other two gave conflicting accounts, now that they had a starting point, Ryu would be able to track down the answer one way or another.

He bent down and swept her into his arms. Kenzie leaned back enough to frown. "What are you doing?"

"I missed you."

"I missed you, too."

Liam slowly set her on her feet. "Have you slept since I saw you last?"

A lie might comfort him, but she didn't have it in her right now. "No. There was too much to do and then..." She shuddered. "I didn't want to dream."

"Come on." He took her hand and towed her into her room and carefully shut the door behind them. "You can sleep now. I'll watch over you."

"Liam." She dug in her heels. "This is going to get ugly. Really ugly. It was bad before, but if that information is accurate, then saying things will get complicated is a vast understatement." He tried to tug her toward him, but she resisted. "You didn't sign on for this."

"Kenzie, I signed on for *you*. I don't give a fuck if the person responsible turns out to be the goddamn Pope. We'll deal with it. End of story."

"You're right." She finally let him pull her to the bed and strip away first her clothes and then his. It was only once they were both tucked into her bed that Kenzie found her words. "I am really, really glad you're here, Liam."

"I have your back, Kenzie. I'll *always* have your back. No matter what this shitshow of a world throws at us, it's me and you."

Me and you.

She cuddled closer to him, breathing him in and letting the heat of his body soak some of the tension from hers. "Me and you against the motherfucking world."

Liam ran his hand down her spine and back up again as if reassuring himself that this was real. She was here and so was he. Kenzie understood the sentiment. She couldn't stop trying to get closer to him, to do something to drive away whatever tomorrow would bring.

She finally relaxed with a slow exhale as the truth settled over her. Liam was here, here with her and here for good. It didn't matter what tomorrow would bring, because they'd rise up and face it.

Together.

* * *

THANK you so much for reading Kenzie and Liam's story! If you enjoyed it, please consider leaving a review.

The Horsemen's story isn't over! The series picks up shortly after the end of HER RIVAL'S TOUCH with HIS

TORMENTED HEART. Ryu's still reeling from the sheer betrayal of their discovery, and while Amarante begins putting a new plan into place, he's forced to contend with her new recruit. Delilah seems far too timid to be at home on the Island of Ys. Touching her is completely out of the question... But every time Ryu is alone in a room with her, he finds himself giving in to temptation Delilah offers. No matter that it might cost the Horsemen everything as a result...

You can also pick up THEIRS FOR THE NIGHT, my FREE novella that goes back to where the Royal Triad of Thalania first began. An exiled prince, his bodyguard, and the bartender they can't quite manage to leave alone.

If you're craving something a little darker and a whole lot sexier, check out DESPERATE MEASURES! It's the first in a brand new series I fondly call Kinky Villains, and answers the question—What if Jafar won and he and Jasmine ended up together? Available now!

Want to stay up to date on my new releases and get exclusive content, including short stories and cover reveals? Be sure to sign up for my newsletter!

Join my Patreon if you'd like to get early copies of my indie titles, as well as a unique short story every month featuring a couple that YOU get to vote on!

ACKNOWLEDGMENTS

A huge thank you to Eagle and Lynda for continuing to help me put together the best versions of my books possible. I couldn't do it without you!

As always, thanks to Lalana, Asa, and Lauren for being my go-tos when times get tough, as they always seem to do about 60% of the way through the book.

Big thanks to every single reader who asked when Liam was getting his own book. Without your persistence, I don't know that I would have found him the perfect story—or the perfect partner. No side character left behind!

Lots of love and smooches to Tim for holding down the household when I get buried in other worlds. Love you like a love song, and I will always pick you up Girl Scout cookies, even when you don't ask for them. I got you, babe!

ABOUT THE AUTHOR

New York Times and USA TODAY bestselling author Katee Robert learned to tell her stories at her grandpa's knee. Her 2015 title, The Marriage Contract, was a RITA finalist, and RT Book Reviews named it 'a compulsively readable book with just the right amount of suspense and tension." When not writing sexy contemporary and romantic suspense, she spends her time playing imaginary games with her children, driving her husband batty with what-if questions, and planning for the inevitable zombie apocalypse.

www.kateerobert.com

Keep up to date on all new release and sale info by joining Katee's NEWSLETTER!

Made in the USA
Columbia, SC
21 January 2025